A Willowdale, Indiana Story

Mrs. Ivey's Café

A Novel

Carla J. Underwood

Mud Pies Press
FOUNTAIN HILLS, ARIZONA

Carla J. Underwood/Mud Pies Press
13235 N. Verde River Dr., #308
Fountain Hills, Arizona 85268
www.mudpiespress.com
carla@mudpiespress.com

Publisher's Note: This is a work of fiction. Names, characters, places and incidents are a product of the author's imagination. Locales and public names are sometimes used for atmospheric purposes. Any resemblance to actual people, living or dead, or to businesses, companies, events, institutions, or locales is completely coincidental.

Cover Design © 2017 by Dawn Underwood
Book Layout © 2014 BookDesignTemplates.com
Cover Layout © 2014 BookDesignTemplates.com

Mrs. Ivey's Café/Carla J. Underwood--1st edition
ISBN 978-0-9978780-0-4

To my family for their love and encouragement

Preface

Small towns similar to Willowdale were common in Indiana in the late 1950's. The residents were hard workers, and their small businesses played many roles in order to provide the basic needs of their town and the surrounding farms.

There was always one place of business in a small town where everyone gathered to celebrate the good times and to comfort one another in bad times. In Willowdale, that place was Ivey's Café.

More and more, their high school graduates attended college. It was expensive, but most of the students worked during the school year or on summer vacations to help pay for their higher education.

For some, a degree meant freedom from a lifetime of work on the farm or in nearby factories. Others returned home to improve family businesses or farms. Whatever they chose to do, their small-town ideals stayed with them. Of those were the respect for strong family bonds, the shared values of the community and the fidelity of lifelong friendships.

Table of Contents

One

"Uh-oh."

It was all I could think to say. My bedroom was tucked up under the eaves on the second floor of the farmhouse, but I could clearly hear the click of Grandma's shoes.

I imagined her pacing back and forth on the wooden landing at the bottom of the stairs, and I was pretty sure about one thing. She was upset. Grandma always paced when she was upset.

"Do you see him, Shirley?"

Her words carried all the way up the stairs, down the hall and through the open door of my room. It was an admirable distance for a small woman with a voice to match, but her question caught me by surprise.

What was she talking about? And why was she shouting? Grandma never shouted. She considered shouting unladylike and impolite in the extreme.

"See who, Grandma?"

"Mr. Martin, of course," she said. "Have you seen Mr. Martin?"

I sucked in a deep breath. Oops. She had asked me to be on the lookout for her handyman because I had a view of the county road. But I was sitting at the desk on the opposite side of the room, and there was no way I could see out the window.

"Not yet," I said.

It wasn't exactly a lie. I really hadn't seen him. But I guess it was a lie of omission since I left out the part about how I forgot what she asked me to do.

Before I had a chance to apologize for my forgetfulness, the clicking stopped. There was a short pause. Then, Grandma's voice faded away.

"If you don't see him in the next five minutes, young lady," she said, "you get yourself down here."

I didn't realize I was holding my breath. I released it in a single gush.

"Okay, Grandma."

Something had her all worked up, and I better do what she asked. Even though I was in Willowdale against my will, being in trouble with Grandma was not how I wanted my summer to start.

When I thought she was out of ear shot, I put my pen down and tore the top sheet of paper off the writing tablet. I couldn't risk taking the time to finish my letter. Instead, I folded it in half and slipped it into a manila envelope in the desk's bottom drawer.

Before Grandma yelled at me, I was so busy writing I didn't realize how chilly the tiny bedroom was so early in the morning. My arms were covered with goose bumps, and my fingers were icy and stiff from holding the pen.

For a few seconds, I rubbed my arms with my cold hands, but that didn't help. I reached over, grabbed the afghan from across the foot of my bed and draped it around my shoulders.

"Grandma," I said. "How did I ever keep from freezing when I used to play with my dolls in here?"

A single shaft of early morning light spilled across the built-in seat below the dormer window. I switched off the desk lamp, crossed the room in four short strides, and plopped down in the meager beam. Hoping to warm up even more, I curled my legs up under my skirt and pulled the afghan tighter.

"I don't know why you're coming here instead of the café, Mr. Martin," I said to myself. "But if you don't get here pretty soon, I'll freeze solid before I even start my first day of work."

I was in the habit of talking to myself. I suppose it had something to do with the fact I was an only child. Who else would I talk to when Mom wasn't around?

I freed my left arm from the woolen cocoon and squinted at my watch. The tiny hands were too faint to read in the dim light, so I tucked my arm back under the afghan and looked outside.

Through the small window I could see over the tops of the front yard trees and as far as the water tower in the center of Willowdale. But in spite of what Grandma thought, only a sliver of the gravel road at the bottom of the hill was visible between the branches of the thick canopy.

She didn't give me any reason why she wanted me to watch for Mr. Martin. All she said was he was coming, and it was important for her to see him before we left for her café. Grandma always had her reasons, so I didn't ask why.

I focused on that one sliver of road at the edge of the corn-field and studied each vehicle headed toward town. Mr. Martin always drove my grandpa's green 1939 Chevrolet truck to run errands, but from that distance and in that light, they all looked a dull brown.

I shook my head in disbelief at my whole situation. Not only did Grandma have me spying out my window, but she was already putting me to work in the café. I only arrived on the train last night. Couldn't I have just one day of rest?

"I shouldn't even be here," I said. "I should be back home in South Bend, going to the beach or having slumber parties with my girlfriends."

"Now, Shirley," my mother had said. "You're the oldest grandchild, and your grandmother needs help."

I tried to argue my way out of spending the summer in Willowdale, but I understood. My grandparents were married for 52 years until Grandpa passed away last fall, and I figured Grandma might be lonely. But, lonely or not, I didn't want to miss out on all the summer fun at home.

"But, Mom," I said. "Why can't she get somebody in Wil-lowdale to help her?"

"Because it's a family matter, and the work experience will be good for you."

"But there's nothing to do there."

"I'm sure your grandmother will keep you busy enough."

I looked straight at her, jutted my lower lip outward and said, "I won't have any friends to help celebrate my sixteenth birthday."

My pout didn't seem to impress Mom. I figured tears wouldn't either, so I tried my most pitiful look. I was certain she would see the situation my way. I was wrong. She didn't.

She took Grandma's letter out of its envelope and waved it in front of me. It was clear Grandma needed me, and there would be no way to refuse her request no matter how much I protested.

"I won't hear any more complaining," she said. "You're going to Willowdale for the summer, and that's all there is to it."

Thanks to my Mom's strict observance of family obligations, I was more than a hundred miles from home. I was all alone in a cold bedroom, studying a dusty road and looking for Grandpa's old truck. The whole situation was absurd, and I was on the verge of tears for real.

"Sure glad my friends can't see me now."

The rhythmic ticking of the alarm clock on the nightstand beside the bed caught my attention. Its glowing hands read six o'clock.

"Mr. Martin," I said. "You might not care about being late and making Grandma mad, but I don't want her mad at me."

I jumped down from the window seat, tossed the afghan on the bed and brushed out a few wrinkles in my wrap-around skirt. I didn't have time to worry about the clothes I picked to wear. I just hoped Grandma would think I was dressed properly for work.

I hurried out of the room and down the hall past the closed doors of three other bedrooms. I could have slept in any one of them, but my old playroom was my favorite.

I practically sprinted toward the staircase. Family photos, framed and hung in a neat row along the wall, passed by me in a blur. Most brought back quick, happy memories.

At the last one, I stopped short. A picture of our only Ivey family reunion showed Grandma and Grandpa, arm in arm, surrounded by all of my cousins and me.

"I sure do miss you, Grandpa."

"Shirley, where are you?"

Grandma's voice sounded far away and a little bit desperate. I spun away from the picture, raced the rest of the way down the hall and tore down the staircase two steps at a time, using the oak banister for balance.

When I reached the wooden landing, I stopped and sniffed the air. The aroma of freshly brewed coffee enveloped me like a warm embrace, and my empty stomach rumbled.

Grandma was fond of saying young people should start the day with a hearty breakfast, but we all knew Grandma's only expertise in the kitchen was brewing coffee. I couldn't begin to imagine what a hearty breakfast meant to her.

"Shirley, I need your help."

As I started for the kitchen, the rich scent of Grandma's coffee was joined by another, less appealing one. Burned toast.

"Shirley?"

"I'm coming, Grandma."

Two

Mr. Martin eased the old truck along the neglected dirt road. While keeping one hand on the wheel, he gripped the shift lever with the other. Potholes, the remnants of countless traffic on the soft soil, spread out ahead of him like dimples on a golf ball.

"Darn county," he said to himself. "When're they gonna fix these things?"

He snaked his way past each hole, forcing the shift lever back and forth between the first and second gears. Each time, the transmission growled in protest.

"Come on, ol' girl," he coaxed the truck. "We're already runnin' late."

As the truck bounced down the road, a dozen glass bottles filled with fresh milk clanked against each other. He reached across the seat, steadied the two metal crates holding the bottles and slowed the truck's speed even more.

"Whoa, there," he said. "Mrs. Ivey don't want her order spilt."

He eased the truck to a stop where the dirt road intersected the county road and forced the gear shift into neutral. With the engine idling, he looked up at Mrs. Ivey's farmhouse.

It was built of grey limestone and surrounded by a dozen hardwood trees. Her husband Robert situated it on a small rise so it towered above the surrounding cornfields. In the early morning light, the windows were like dark, unblinking eyes staring back at him.

He knew Robert built the farmhouse out of the stone because he wanted to protect his family from tornadoes. And his plan worked. Willowdale was situated in the heart of tornado alley, but not one of them ever threatened the old house.

He shook his head. He hadn't thought of that in years, and he didn't know why he thought of it then. He figured it might have something to do with Mrs. Ivey's phone call.

It confused him. She had never bothered him at home before, and he couldn't imagine what her call was really about.

"I need to talk to you first thing tomorrow morning," she had said.

"Well, Mrs. Ivey, we could visit some when I git the milk ta the café."

"No, my granddaughter will be there, and I don't want her to overhear what I have to say."

"I guess I can stop by yer house on the way ta town."

"Good. Meet me in the driveway."

That was it. No explanation. In order to get to her house before going to the café, he was forced to drive on the dirt road from Monticello. He knew the milk needed to be put in the cooler right away to keep it from spoiling, and he couldn't imagine what was more important than that. Besides, it was a huge departure from his normal routine, and he didn't much care for his routine being interrupted.

"This better be real important," he said and pulled the truck onto the county road.

If she weren't Robert's widow, he might have given her a piece of his mind, but she was a no-nonsense kind of woman. He knew she wouldn't abide anybody, not even her husband's oldest friend, telling her what he thought about how she ran her business.

"No, sir," he said. "I just gotta put up with how she does things."

He was tired and certainly old enough to retire, but he couldn't afford it. After paying his wife's medical bills, the gas for all the trips back and forth to the hospital and her funeral expenses, his savings account was empty.

"The way I see it, I'm gonna die of old age right here in this truck runnin' an errand fer Mrs. Ivey."

Three

On my way to the kitchen, I passed by the room Grandma called the parlor. Mom and I called it the living room, but Grandma was part of the older generation. She was used to things being more formal.

Nothing in the room was changed. There were the same area rugs on the dark hardwood floor, the same overstuffed furniture and the same dark molding around the windows and doors. Even the cabinet next to Grandpa's leather chair still held his Philco radio.

"Oh, no," I said. "No television?"

Aunt Maude had bought the first set in Willowdale, and Grandpa told me how the whole town paraded through her general store to see it. He wanted to buy one, too, but Grandma wouldn't hear of it.

"I absolutely forbid you to bring one of those horrible things into this house."

"But it's for the grandchildren when they come to visit."

"Not my grandchildren," she said. "Whatever is this world coming to?"

Thank goodness I loved to read. That was my main source of entertainment when Mom and I visited at Thanksgiving and

Christmas. A quick glance told me the same books I read over all those years still filled the bookcases flanking the fireplace.

"Shirley."

Grandma's voice sounded tense, so I picked up my pace. I hurried through the vestibule, Grandma's word for entry hall with its heavy oak door and lead glass windows, and I rushed past the formal dining room with its crystal chandelier and bay window.

Every room sported dark hardwood floors and identical brocade drapes at the windows. They gave the house a warm appearance, but the air was chilled down there, too. My arms were covered in goose bumps again.

No matter how cold it was, I knew Grandma would never spend the money to pay for a coal shipment so late in the spring, and there was no sense in me complaining. I would have to adjust to it or wear sweaters inside the house until the weather turned warmer.

"Never be wasteful," Grandma always said. "If you watch your pennies, the dimes will take care of themselves."

"Well, Grandma," I said. "The way you watch your pennies, you must have lots of dimes by now."

"Shirley!"

Although I was running by the time I reached the kitchen, the room was nearly filled with smoke. Grandma was at the window over the sink and shrouded in a grey cloud. It was headed my way, threatening to spill into the rest of the house.

"Oh, boy."

I kicked at a rubber doorstop, and the door separating the kitchen from the rest of the house slammed closed behind me. When Grandma turned her head toward me, her face was flushed.

"What kept you?" she said. "I need your help over here."

Without a moment's hesitation, I ran to the window and pulled up hard on the bottom sash. Grandma beat on the wooden frame with the heel of her hand at the same time, but the yellow bead of caulk on the sill refused to give way.

"Pull up harder, Shirley."

I groaned from my efforts, and Grandma beat even harder until her face turned bright red. After we struggled for a minute or two, there was a loud pop. The caulking released its grip, and the window slid up the casing with a bang.

With the window up and the smoke oozing out of it, we poked our heads through the opening, coughing through the smoke and stench. Thankfully, Grandma's normally pale skin became less red with each breath she took. Only then did I stop worrying what I would do if she keeled over with a heart attack.

"I guess your grandpa used a little too much calking."

I chuckled to myself. It was obvious from the glob of chalking left on the windowsill that Grandpa had over done it.

"What now, Grandma?"

"A little more ventilation should do the trick."

I stayed at the open window gulping fresh air while Grandma hurried to the back door. She swung it wide open, and the remaining smoke escaped through the screen door into the clear June air.

"Well, young lady," she said, jamming her fists on her hips. "If you had been down here sooner to help me, this would never have happened."

"Grandma?"

"You know how awful I am at cooking."

I glanced over at the kitchen table and studied a stack of charred bread on a china serving platter. It looked more like a pile of coal clinkers than toast. But as unappetizing as they looked, I was proud of Grandma for at least trying to cook breakfast for us.

"I'm sorry I took so long," I said, stifling a grin. "I'll help with breakfast tomorrow."

"I should hope so," she said. "Your mother raised you to be more considerate than this."

I felt the color rise in my cheeks. Why did she think I could be upstairs looking out the window for Mr. Martin and be down in the kitchen cooking breakfast at the same time? I really wanted to know, but I held my tongue. My mother really did raise me to be considerate and respectful of my elders.

My anger eased a little when the sound of tires crunching along the gravel driveway drifted in through the open window. I could actually feel the flush on my face disappear.

"Mr. Martin must be here," I said.

Before the familiar ping of the old truck's engine ceased, Grandma bolted outside. I started to follow, but she waved her hand at me.

"You stay there while I discuss something with Mr. Martin."

A few tears clouded my vision. I couldn't say if they were from the smoke irritating my eyes or from being excluded. Either way, I grabbed one of the linen napkins off the table.

While I wiped the tears away, I stood at the window and watched Mr. Martin step out of the truck. He wore his usual khaki pants, faded blue shirt and the old felt hat he was wearing the last time I saw him.

"Ye gods and little fishes, Mr. Martin," Grandma said. "Why haven't you delivered my milk order to the café?"

She hugged herself against the cool Indiana morning and looked toward the truck. I followed her gaze and saw two crates of milk bottles on the front seat.

"I came by here first," he said. "Just like ya asked."

Grandma stuffed her hands into the pockets on the sides of her dress and stiffened her back. She glanced in my direction.

"I did no such thing," she said. "You must be mistaken."

Mr. Martin slipped the weathered hat from his head. He dug into his pants pocket, pulled out a crumpled handkerchief and wiped at the inside of the hatband.

"Yes, ma'am, but—" he started to say.

Before he could finish, Grandma stepped closer to him and lowered her voice. I strained to hear what she said, but I couldn't quite make out the words.

Mr. Martin nodded his head and looked in my direction. When our eyes met, he glared at me.

That's odd, I thought, acknowledging Mr. Martin with a quick wave. What do you suppose that's all about?

When their hushed conversation ended, Mr. Martin stopped wiping at the hatband. He wadded the handkerchief into a ball and stuffed it back inside his pocket.

"Now, you get that milk into the cooler and do what I asked," Grandma said, taking a step back. "Do you understand?"

"Yes, ma'am," he said. "I'll git right on it."

He slid the hat on his head and walked back to the truck. I heard him grumble something under his breath.

Grandma must not have heard what he said because she turned around without answering him. She came back into the house, pulled two sweaters off the hooks beside the back door and handed one to me.

"Put this on," she said. "There's no time for breakfast now."

I took the sweater from her and slipped my arms into the sleeves. I was grateful for the warmth, but I was totally confused.

"Why did Mr. Martin come here this morning, Grandma?"

"It's nothing for you to worry about, dear," she said. "It's just business."

"Business?"

"Yes, business."

Grandma pulled her sweater over her work dress and fastened the top button. From her stern expression and her tight jaw, I knew I shouldn't ask more questions.

"And don't worry about fixing supper tonight," she said. "Aunt Maude will make something for us."

"Okay."

I didn't realize I was expected to help with all the meals. I knew how to fix breakfast, but I didn't have much experience at cooking supper. With Mom's help I made a decent meat loaf and a passable spaghetti sauce, but that was it. Mom was the cook at our house.

Grandma jutted her chin upward, pushed the screen door open and hurried off the back porch. Talking over her shoulder as she went, she reminded me of one of her cardinal rules.

"I have never opened the café late, young lady, and I am not about to begin today."

Before following her outside, I glanced back at the kitchen table and the uneaten toast. My stomach ached from hunger, and it betrayed me with a loud growl.

"Grandma," I said, forcing the idea of breakfast out of my mind. "Don't you want to lock the door?"

Without slowing her stride she said, "Whatever for?"

Four

Mr. Martin steered the old truck back down the serpentine driveway beside the old farmhouse and stopped at the county road. When the dust settled after the last of the traffic passed by, he eased onto the gravel road and shifted through the protesting gears.

"What was that about?" he said to himself. "Mrs. Ivey whisperin' an' wantin' me ta call her friends ta meet her as soon as the café's closed?"

The old truck kicked up enough dust to blow in through the driver's window, so he cranked it shut. Steering with one hand, he reached across the milk crates and rolled up the passenger window, too.

"I promised yer husband I'd look out fer ya, Mrs. Ivey," he said. "But I didn't think it'd mean sneakin' around."

Once he reached the first paved street in Willowdale, the truck no longer kicked up dust, and he rolled the driver's window down again. He rested his cocked elbow on the door frame and breathed in the morning air.

"Nope, I sure never promised ta sneak around or call a secret meetin'," he said. "An' ya said somethin' about it bein' a surprise fer Shirley?"

When he turned onto Main Street, he stopped at the filling station to borrow the owner's phone. He knew Earl wouldn't mind if he made a few calls as long as they were important. He couldn't think of anything more important than keeping Mrs. Ivey happy.

Once he finished calling everyone about the meeting, he bought five gallons of gas and continued driving up Main Street. At 1st Street he turned left, circled around to the alley and brought the truck to a stop at the rear door of Ivey's Café.

"So," he said. "If it's fer Shirley, ya figure we'll all do whatever ya want."

He eased out of the truck and walked around to the passenger door. Both metal crates were still upright, and none of the bottles was broken. He reached in, hefted the closest crate off the seat and turned toward the café.

"Guess I don't have a choice if I wanna keep my job."

He paused at the rear door to rest and to take several deep breaths. He didn't remember a few bottles of milk weighing so much.

"I'm doin' this fer Robert 'cause Shirley's his granddaughter," he said. "But that don't mean I have ta like it."

Five

The traffic was heavy on the county road, raising clouds of dust. Thankfully, there was a slight breeze to keep it away from us, and the grass and weeds growing along the edge of the road gave Grandma and me a fairly soft path under foot.

The café was still nearly a mile away once we left the end of the driveway, but Grandma didn't seem to want to talk. I matched her hurried pace, step for step, without speaking.

After several minutes of silence, I literally felt Grandma's tension evaporate. I peeked over at her. Her jaw was slack, and her lips were turned up into a slight grin.

"It sure is a beautiful day," I said. "Don't you think so, Grandma?"

"Yes, I do."

When she didn't elaborate, I struggled to find a better subject. I decided to talk about what I knew best.

"If I was at home this summer, I'd be going to camp or taking trips to the beach."

"If I were home, not was," she corrected me, "and we have the beach at Lake Sullivan."

"It's not quite the same as Lake Michigan or even the lakes close to home."

"No, it isn't."

"I mean, Lake Sullivan doesn't have all those big waves or the sand dunes like Lake Michigan."

Grandma stared straight ahead. Her pace never slowed.

"You don't need large waves or sand dunes to enjoy a swim," she said.

"No, I guess I don't."

Again, we walked in silence. When we reached the first few houses on the edge of Willowdale, I watched the town around us come alive. It wasn't as bustling as my hometown, but it definitely bustled.

Farm trucks of every description passed by, and several of the drivers honked and waved at us. I waved back at them, but Grandma looked straight ahead. She only nodded at them in acknowledgement.

That part of town had no curbs or sidewalks, but the huge lawns around the modest bungalows were neatly trimmed. Every yard boasted a maple or elm or even a willow tree. I had to admit Willowdale was a beautiful little town in late spring.

Although I enjoyed seeing the town again, the longer we walked, the sorer my feet got. The thin leather soles on the dress flats I wore were poor protection against the sharp gravel poking up between the trampled weeds and grass.

"Grandma," I said, thinking I'd found the perfect solution to my sore feet. "Why don't you drive Grandpa's truck to work?"

"Your grandfather gave his truck to Mr. Martin to run errands, not to take me to work."

"I'm sure Mr. Martin wouldn't mind if you used your own truck once in a while."

"That isn't it."

I followed Grandma's lead and stepped around a protruding thistle. Its thorns threatened to snag our skirts.

"What is it then?"

"I don't know how to drive."

I shook my head, and my pony tail wagged back and forth. That was big news.

"Wow. I thought all grownups knew how to drive."

"Well, I am one who doesn't."

I ignored the traffic passing us and studied Grandma's face. I thought she was joking, and I waited for her to laugh. She didn't.

"Neither my father nor your grandfather believed women were capable of operating such mechanical devices."

I laughed and shook my head again, but Grandma didn't crack a smile. She looked straight ahead, her jaw tight again.

Oops, I thought. She's serious.

We walked in silence once more until we reached the first sidewalk in Willowdale. The scattered bungalows with the large yards gave way to paved streets and ranch style houses on small lots.

"But, Grandma," I said, stepping up onto the walk. "Why would they think that?"

"They believed you shouldn't operate something you don't know how to repair."

"That's silly," I said. "None of the girls back home know how to fix a car."

"It was more than that."

"More?"

"They didn't think it was appropriate for a successful businessman's wife to drive."

We walked without speaking for another minute or two. Then, I wanted to know more. No, I needed to know more.

"I don't understand why it wouldn't be—appropriate."

"Because," she said. "They believed a successful businessman would only appear successful if he could afford to hire someone to do the driving."

Hire it done. So that's why Mr. Martin always had the truck and ran all the errands. He wasn't just Grandpa's friend, he was hired help.

I did a quick hop-step and touched Grandma's arm. A solution to my sore feet problem was still within reach.

"Grandma," I said. "Mom's been teaching me to drive."

"I see."

"She says I just need a little more practice, and I'll be ready to get my license."

"That's nice," she said. "It's always important to practice your skills."

I looked over at Grandma and studied her face. I thought it was the perfect time to press my agenda, so I jumped at the opportunity.

"But, Grandma," I said. "That means I can get my driver's license when I turn sixteen next month."

My head was reeling with all the possibilities. To get my license was my dream. Besides, my friends would really be jealous when I got back home.

"That certainly is something to look forward to someday, my dear."

"If I get my license, I can do the driving, and we can ride to work."

"No, dear."

I thought Grandma would explain why she didn't want me to get my license. Instead, she picked up her pace. Not even the occasional crack or bulge in the concrete walk slowed her, and I struggled to keep up.

"Why not?"

"It's Mr. Martin's job to drive for me, and he needs the truck at all times to run errands whenever I need something," she said. "Besides, walking is good exercise."

We'll see about that, Grandma, I thought. We'll just see about that.

In another few minutes, we turned onto Main Street, and I couldn't believe my eyes. It seemed as though nothing had changed since the last time I visited Grandma. It still looked like a scene from the 1920's, not 1957.

The entire business district consisted of two short blocks of single story, red brick buildings on one side of the street. On the other side, there was one long block of wood framed buildings. Some single story. Some with attic space on top. 1st and 2nd Streets dead ended at Main Street and led to the rest of the downtown and some of the oldest houses.

Grandma's Ivey's Café stood in the center of the first short block next to a vacant lot. Aunt Maude's general store was diagonally across the street. It had attic space on top.

The buildings reminded me of strings of broken beads. One neglected façade was lined up alongside the next. To make things worse, among the active businesses were some unoccupied stores. I remembered one of them used to be a beauty shop.

But no movie theater, I thought. I told Mom there wouldn't be anything to do.

I kept my disappointment to myself and stared straight ahead. It appeared my only hope to alleviate certain boredom was to rekindle an old friendship.

"I can hardly wait to see Liz again."

"That won't be possible, my dear."

My jaw dropped. I looked over at her and waited for an explanation.

"Her father sold the mill, and her family moved to Lafayette."

I took a deep breath and slowly exhaled as though my lungs were two deflating balloons. I just knew I wouldn't have any fun without Liz. I wanted to scream and stamp my feet. I didn't.

Behind the café, the wooden water tower I saw from my bedroom window loomed over the tiny downtown. The Willowdale lettering on its side was faded and barely legible. The poor thing looked as sad as I felt.

"See our new awning?" Grandma said. "And the screen door your grandfather put on?"

I saw the pride on her face and made no comment about the meager improvements. Instead, I searched for something positive to say.

"Maybe I can make enough money this summer to buy a class ring and sweater."

Grandma picked up the pace even more. In spite of my longer legs, I struggled to keep up with her.

"So, you want a ring and a sweater."

"Everyone will be wearing them."

"Are they really necessary?"

"Necessary?"

While I struggled to find a better reply, we stopped at the curb and waited for the traffic to pass. Just before we stepped into the street to cross over to the café, the high-pitched, metallic sound of a bicycle bell rang out.

"Ye gods and little fishes."

A boy sped past us on a Schwinn bike, missing us by only inches. He went by in such a hurry I only had time to notice his faded denim jacket and two empty saddlebags across the bike's rear fender.

"Young man," Grandma said. "You stop that bicycle right this minute!"

"Sorry, Mrs. Ivey," he called over his shoulder. "I'm running a little late."

He pedaled down the street without slowing and rang the bike's bell at every person on the sidewalk as he passed by. At

1st Street, he took a sliding turn to the left and disappeared around the corner.

"Who was that, Grandma?"

"Jimmy Spencer," she said. "His father bought the old mill."

"How old is he?"

"I don't know," she said. "I suppose he's about your age."

"Perfect."

I couldn't help but smile at the possibility of meeting a new friend, but Grandma gave me one of her stern looks. When she spoke, there was no humor in her voice.

"You listen to me," she said. "You are much too young to be concerned with boys."

That was that. No discussion. She simply took hold of my elbow and led me across the street.

Six

We arrived at the café several minutes before the official opening time, and Grandma hurried me inside. After we hung our sweaters on hooks beside the magazine rack, she locked the door behind us and led me to the front of the dining room.

The place looked just the way it did the last time I was there. Even the Monday special on the menu board behind the lunch counter was the same as it was every Monday I could remember. "Sloppy Joes with Coleslaw and French fries" was scribbled in white chalk.

"Sit down, please," Grandma said, motioning toward the round table at the front of the room.

We walked over to it, and she sat down on one of the hard wooden chairs. Just as I remembered, all the chairs around the table were bare except for the one with a faded green cushion. It was indented with the shape of Grandpa's derriere. A testament to the countless hours he spent working on the café's ledger there.

Respecting his memory, I sat across from Grandma on one of the other hard wooden chairs. I leaned against the stiff backrest and waited for my working orders.

A dull pain radiating from my knees down to the soles of my feet caught my immediate attention. I guessed the blood was once more flowing into my tortured feet. But dull or not, it was pain. All I wanted to do at that moment was kick off my shoes and put my feet up on the seat of one of the other chairs. Of course, I didn't.

The longer I sat waiting for Grandma to speak, the deeper the horizontal strips of wood on the backrest cut into my shoulder blades. I hid all of my discomfort from Grandma with a smile and tried not to wiggle too much.

Grandma didn't seem to notice me or my discomfort. She sat straight in her chair and tucked loose strands of her grey hair back into the bun at the nape of her neck. Then, she tapped her finger against a sheet of paper on the table.

"Shirley," she said. "You'll have several duties to perform."

"Okay."

"I have made a list of them for you."

She pushed the paper toward me, and I read down the list. My duties included busing tables, keeping the magazine and newspaper racks organized, running to the post office inside Aunt Maude's general store and doing other miscellaneous jobs as they became necessary.

"Your workday begins at seven o'clock when the café opens for breakfast," she said. "And your workday ends at three o'clock when the café closes after lunch."

"Okay."

I shifted my weight on the chair and fought the urge to jump up. My legs tingled from the discomfort of the hard seat, and they practically screamed at me to find a more comfortable position. My aching feet and sore back seemed less important and secondary to the new pain.

"The only day we won't open the cafe is on Sunday when none of the businesses are open."

"Okay."

She paused for a moment. Her eyes peered directly into mine.

"I don't ordinarily open for holidays."

"Oh?"

"Except for one," she said. "We'll open for a short time for customers to buy sack lunches on the Fourth of July."

Oh, no, I thought. That's my birthday. I figured she was too busy to remember, but I wouldn't be the one to remind her. That would be disrespectful, and we both knew I was taught better than that.

"Is there a problem, dear?"

I looked down at the list. It seemed pretty complete except for that one oversight.

"No, Grandma, I guess not."

After that, I barely heard her drone on and on with detailed instructions. It was difficult for me to concentrate while imagining a birthday without my friends or a party.

Only pretending to listen, I glanced over Grandma's shoulder and out the large front window. The street was crowded with trucks. Now and then, one and then another pulled in and out of the diagonal parking spaces in front of the café.

41

Several families crossed back and forth from one side of the street to the other. But Jimmy, the one person I hoped to see, didn't go by.

When I didn't see anyone I recognized, I turned my attention back to Grandma. Her instructions seemed to go on forever, and my physical discomfort became unbearable.

"Remember," she said. "If you see something needs to be done, don't wait to be told to do it."

"Okay."

"As your grandfather always said, 'If there's time to lean, there's time to clean'."

She continued explaining my duties, but my mind wandered again. I thought of Jimmy.

I didn't understand why Grandma thought I was too young to think about boys. Lots of my friends were already dating, but I wasn't thinking about dating Jimmy or anyone else. I just needed a friend and someone my age to talk to. How else was I going to survive my stay in Willowdale?

"And always remember, I expect you to be pleasant and helpful at all times."

"Yes, Grandma."

I rested my elbows on the edge of the table and propped my chin in the palms of my hands. Just the idea of spending the summer there and working in the café made me tired.

"Are there any questions, Shirley?"

I wanted to ask her how she could forget my birthday and how I was supposed to have fun without any of my friends. But I was sent there to help Grandma, not hurt her feelings.

"Shirley?"

"No, Grandma," I said, dropping my hands to my lap. "No questions."

"Then, it's time to go to work."

Seven

After delivering the milk and storing the bottles in the walk-in cooler behind the kitchen, Mr. Martin stacked the two crates in a corner of the storeroom at the rear of the café. As always, they would stay right there until his next shopping trip to Monticello.

He could hear Irene in the kitchen prepping food for the breakfast crowd. It was her busiest time of the day at the café, and he didn't want to bother her. Instead of stopping to talk, he tiptoed past the kitchen door and moved as quietly as he could toward the back entrance.

"Mr. Martin," she said. "Are you sneakin' out without sayin' hello?"

He stopped and turned around. The cook was standing at the sink. She was wielding a paring knife and peeling potatoes under a running faucet.

"I wasn't sneakin'."

"Sure hope not," she said. "I need you to run over to Aunt Maude's and get me some more onions."

He knew getting the milk delivery done was only the beginning of his workday. It seemed as though Irene always needed something. If she didn't need milk, it was potatoes she wanted. If she had plenty of potatoes, she ran out of eggs. And on and on it went.

"That all ya want?" he said.

"For now."

Some of the time, Aunt Maude had enough in stock at her general store to cover a shortfall at the café. Most of the time, however, it required him to interrupt his routine, jump into Robert's old truck and make an emergency run to Monticello.

He wanted to tell Irene and Mrs. Ivey they should be able to plan their shopping better than that. The way Robert used to do. But he knew he could never make that suggestion. It would most likely upset both of them, and it would most certainly get him fired.

"No, sir," he said under his breath. "Gittin' in trouble with those two women isn't my job."

"Did you say somethin'?" Irene said, shouting to be heard over the running water.

"I said I'll git the onions."

"I'd appreciate it."

Mr. Martin knew Irene wouldn't be happy if she knew he had another stop to make first, so he quickly turned and walked to the back door. From there, he could hear Mrs. Ivey explaining to Shirley about her duties and obligations.

"Typical city girl," he said. "Never had a job an' don't know the first thing about nothin'."

He shook his head in disgust, put on his crumpled hat and slipped out the door. Because Mrs. Ivey didn't want her granddaughter to know what he was up to, he hoisted himself onto the front seat and slowly backed the truck away from the café. He eased off a little on the gas so the engine didn't ping quite so much, but nothing he did disguised the noise completely.

"Maybe they're talkin' so much they can't hear this old thing anyways."

To be sure he wasn't seen by anyone, he drove down the alley, crossed over 1st Street and continued down the alley to 2nd Street. He pulled the truck into the paved parking lot of the First Community Church and drove to the back of the building. He parked in front of the Sunday school entrance where he was certain the truck wouldn't be spotted by anyone going in or out of the café.

"Shirley shouldn't be able ta see this old thing from here," he said.

Pastor Lawrence opened the door at the first knock and motioned for Mr. Martin to enter. Before he went inside, he removed his hat and scanned the parking lot one last time. When he was satisfied no one saw him arrive, he slipped inside and followed the pastor through the church.

He was led to a large meeting room located behind the sanctuary. At one end of the room, a long table covered with a checkered cloth was outfitted with a coffee pot, china cups and plates, paper napkins and a platter heaped with Aunt Maude's chocolate chip cookies. Radiating out beyond the table were three rows of folding chairs arranged so there was a single aisle down the center.

"Is this what Mrs. Ivey had in mind?"

Mr. Martin nodded in approval. He marveled at how fast the church's social committee managed to put everything together. It was less than an hour since he called everyone from the filling station.

"Thanks for allowin' us ta meet here on such short notice, Pastor," he said.

"All our neighbors are welcome here anytime."

"That's real kind of ya," he said, running his hands along the brim of his hat. "Mrs. Ivey made the meetin' this afternoon sound real important."

"We're happy to help."

As he turned to leave, Pastor Lawrence pointed to the refreshment table and let out a chuckle. Two of the cookies on the platter in the center of the table had fallen onto the table-cloth.

"Well, now," the pastor said. "That looks like a sign to me."

Without any further explanation, he took two napkins and wrapped a cookie in each. He handed Mr. Martin the largest one.

"It's definitely a sign these two errant cookies are meant for us."

Mr. Martin wasn't sure what he meant by errant, but he was relieved to learn the young man had a sense of humor. Even though he hadn't been to a church service since his wife's funeral, he felt at ease with the new pastor. Maybe he would go to church again someday to hear what else the man had to say.

"An' don't ya worry none, Pastor," he said with his mouth full of the cookie. "We'll clean up after an' lock up when we're done."

Eight

By the time Grandma finished instructing me on my duties and the intricacies of the café, a group of customers was congregated outside. I stayed at the table while Grandma went to the front door and unlocked it. When she swung the door open, her customers filed in, and she greeted each one by name.

I guess Grandma knows everybody in town, I thought. But is it going to be this busy every morning?

On their way in, a few customers grabbed a newspaper or a magazine from the rack by the front door. Some sat on the padded stools at the lunch counter, and the rest chose to sit at the tables with the hard wooden chairs.

I looked around, curious to know why so many people would flock there so early in the morning. Then, it hit me. It wasn't just a café. It was also the town's newsstand and a bus stop all rolled into one.

"Wow, Grandma," I said under my breath. "You really are something to run all of this by yourself."

A man in bib overalls stood by the front door and waved a newspaper in the air. I could see from his expression he was upset about something.

"Hey, Mrs. Ivey," he said. "This here paper is yesterday's."

Grandma, already halfway to the kitchen, stopped and spun around. She hurried over to the newspaper rack and rummaged through the entire stack of papers.

"Ye gods," she said. "Where is that boy?"

I had no idea who she was talking about, so I took the opportunity to peel myself off the chair. As far as I was concerned, its only purpose was to torture and maim.

Thankfully, the pain in my back and legs eased when I stood up, but my feet still ached. It was then I vowed, if I managed to live through the day, to throw my dress flats in the garbage.

I watched Grandma as she discussed the irresponsibility of young people with the man in the bib overalls. While she talked, she reached behind the lunch counter and grabbed a white cotton apron. Once it was tied in place, she looked the way I always remembered. She was all business in her navy blue work dress, her white apron and her laced shoes.

Without a pause, she poured a fresh cup of coffee and placed it in front of the distraught bib overalls man. After a few swallows, he seemed calmer, but he still rambled on about irresponsible young people. I decided my best move was to get out of his verbal line of fire and go to the kitchen.

The cook, a short, rotund woman, was chopping potatoes and onions on a cutting board next to the sink. Although she seemed too preoccupied with preparations to notice me, she looked up and flashed a wide, somewhat toothless smile in my direction.

"Why, you must be Shirley," she said. "You're practically the spittin' image of your daddy."

I didn't know what to think. Nobody ever said that to me before, but I took it as a compliment. In all the pictures Mom showed me, my father had been an extraordinarily attractive man.

"Good morning," I said.

"By the way, I'm Irene," she said. "Sorry I can't give you a proper welcome hug with these dirty hands of mine."

"That's okay."

"I'll just make it up to you later."

"Okay."

I was relieved to have dodged the hug. It was one of the most annoying small-town rituals I knew, and I really hoped she'd forget all about it.

Without skipping a beat, she went back to chopping more potatoes and onions, and I scanned the kitchen for something to keep myself busy. A carafe of coffee on the warming plate caught my attention.

Although serving coffee wasn't one of my official duties, Grandma wanted me to do whatever needed to be done. I grabbed the carafe, left the relative quiet of the kitchen and re-entered the din in the dining room.

"Thanks, sweetie," one of the women said after I filled her coffee cup. "You keep that high octane coming."

I continued to circulate through the dining room, and the discussion about my generation was over. The bib overalls man was eating his breakfast, and Grandma was talking with a man and woman seated at one of the small tables.

While I moved from table to table with the carafe, I kept a wary eye on a woman dressed in a flowing skirt and high heels talking on the telephone at the end of the counter. She appeared to be oblivious to the sign taped on the wall beside her. It read "For business and emergency use only", and I was pretty sure her call was personal when she called the person on the other end of the line "darling".

Behind the woman, a man in ragged jeans and a cowboy hat tacked a notice to a bulletin board on the back wall. I wondered if his small piece of paper would ever be seen among the jumble of other notes.

I walked around the room for several more minutes sur-rounded by the smells of Irene's fried bacon, freshly baked biscuits and hashed potatoes with onions. The mouth-watering odors reminded me just how hungry I was, and my stomach let out a loud grumble.

Oh, boy, I thought. Before I have a chance to die of bore-dom this summer, I'll probably starve to death.

To distract myself from the ache in my stomach, I took the carafe back to the kitchen. I exchanged it for a wet rag and began cleaning one of the vacated tables. The jumble of voic-es in the dining room was pretty loud, but I still heard the familiar click of Grandma's shoes. The clicking was close behind me and getting closer.

"Shirley, I wouldn't ordinarily recommend you eat in front of my customers."

I looked up from the table I was scrubbing and turned around. There stood Grandma with a plate heaped with food in one hand and a glass of milk in the other.

"Wow, Grandma, is all that for me?"

"Yes, dear. I thought you might be a little hungry."

I plopped down on the nearest chair, ignoring the hardness of the seat. It felt so good to get off my feet I let out a long, low moan.

"This should help cheer you up," she said.

My mouth watered at the sight of scrambled eggs and bacon. Two slices of golden brown toast, glistening with melted butter, lay neatly along the edge of the plate.

"Did you make the toast, Grandma?"

I smiled at her. I knew full well Irene was the one in charge of the kitchen. Grandma didn't exactly smile back at me, but I thought I detected a slight upward curve to her lips.

"Now, now, we'll have none of that, young lady."

She placed the dish of food and the glass of milk on the table in front of me. From her apron pocket, she retrieved a knife and fork and handed them to me with great fanfare.

"Thank you," I said.

"You are most welcome."

I dug right in. Even before Grandma had time to return to the cash register, I polished off the eggs and started on the bacon.

Some of the customers gave me sidelong glances, but that didn't stop me from devouring the rest of the food. I didn't look up from the plate until I heard the screen door shut with a bang.

There was Jimmy Spencer, the boy who practically ran us down on our way to work. He stood just inside the door with his arms full of folded newspapers.

"Morning, Mrs. Ivey."

He dropped the bundle of papers on the floor in front of the magazine rack and watched Grandma at the counter. Without another word, he shifted his weight from one foot to the other and waited.

Grandma opened the cash register and counted out a handful of coins. She slammed the drawer closed, counted the coins one more time and stomped over to Jimmy.

"You're late, young man," she said.

"Yes, ma'am."

He pulled off his baseball cap and glanced from Grandma to the stack of papers and back again. When Grandma didn't say more, he wiped off his hand on his faded jeans and combed through his disheveled hair with his fingers. It didn't help. The thick, blonde curls immediately fell back down in front of his eyes.

"You tell your father you need a haircut."

"Yes, ma'am."

Her tone was so cold I visualized icicles clinging to every word, but Jimmy never flinched. He stood his ground and returned Grandma's stare.

"Are they all there?" she said, nodding toward the stack of papers.

"Yes, ma'am," he said. "I counted them twice to make sure."

Grandma leaned down and counted the papers in the bundle. With a short huff, she stood up and glared at him.

"That's fine," she said, handing him the money. "But I trust you won't be late tomorrow."

"No, ma'am."

Grandma turned her attention to the customers at the counter and left Jimmy standing alone. While her back was toward him, he stuffed the money into his pants pocket.

He started for the door, but before he got there, I caught his eye. The frown he wore for Grandma changed to a wide grin, and he came to an abrupt halt.

"Hi," he said. "You must be Shirley."

"And you must be Jimmy."

"Jim."

"What?"

"I like being called Jim."

"Okay," I said, shrugging my shoulders.

We both looked back at the counter. Grandma was watching us. There was a scowl on her face that could send shivers up the bravest soul's spine. Jim whipped his head back around.

"I'd better get going."

"Sorry about Grandma," I said. "I don't understand what's gotten into her today."

"Oh, she just wants me to remember who the boss is," he said. "And it isn't me."

He glanced over at Grandma again and waved. She returned his gesture with the same scowl.

"See you tomorrow, Mrs. Ivey."

He jammed his cap on his head and made a dash out the door. Just the way he did when he entered, he let the screen door slam shut behind him.

I ran to the front window and watched him climb onto his bike and pedal away. Unlike earlier, the two saddlebags draped over the rear fender were bulging with rolled up newspapers.

"Shirley."

When I looked over at Grandma, she was still standing by the counter and still scowling. She nodded her head in the direction of the magazine rack.

I took the hint and went to the bundle of newspapers Jim left on the floor. I untied the strand of twine holding them together and, one by one, arranged the papers next to the magazines.

As I pulled the old issues from the rack, a small article at the bottom of the front page caught my eye. It touted a Fourth of July fireworks display.

At least somebody's going to have a fun holiday, I thought.

Before I could finish reading the entire piece, an older man at the counter pointed at me with his fork. I could barely understand him as he spoke to me around a mouthful of food.

"Hey, kid," he said. "Bring me one of them new papers."

Since making the customers happy was one of Grandma's rules, I stopped reading and dropped the paper on the floor with the rest of the old editions. I grabbed one of the new papers off the rack and carried it over to him.

"Thanks," he said.

For a second, I was mesmerized by a drop of egg yolk stuck to the man's unshaven chin. I knew it was impolite to stare, but since I didn't know if I should say something or not, I didn't say anything.

"What's the matter with you, kid?" he said.

"Nothing."

"Well, go about your business."

"Okay."

I stepped back a little and waited while Grandma finished adding the cost of the paper to the man's bill. When she finished, she moved out from behind the counter, wiping her hands on the front of her apron. This time, there was a look of concern on her face.

Gee whiz, I thought. Now what did I do?

I scanned the room and tried to figure out what was wrong. When I spotted the dirty dishes and the wet rag I left on the table where I ate, I wasted no time. Under her watchful eye, I hurried to the table and scooped up everything.

Just as I was about to duck into the kitchen with my dirty dishes, I caught a glimpse of Mr. Martin out of the corner of my eye. His back was turned toward me, and the stack of old newspapers I left by the magazine rack was tucked under his arm.

Oh, no, I thought. Grandma will probably be mad at me for not finishing that job either.

In front of me, the percolator on the stove rumbled to life. I stared at it for a few moments, watching the dark liquid bubble up into the clear glass knob on the lid. I was exhausted, my feet hurt and I wished, with all my heart, the day would end. But it was only eight o'clock.

"Shirley?"

The sound of my name came from behind me, and I turned toward the back door. Mr. Martin stood there, his hat in one hand and the old newspapers under his arm.

"I was supposed to take care of the papers," I said without offering so much as a thank you.

"Didn't mean ta over step," he said. "I'll go put 'em in the truck."

Before I could say anything else, he put on his hat and shoved his way out the door. A ring of keys dangling from his belt jingled with his every step.

Nine

When three o'clock finally came, I sat down at one of the small tables and watched Grandma usher the last customer out the door.

I can't believe you do this every day, I thought. Well, every day except Sundays and holidays.

"Of course, that doesn't include the Fourth of July, does it?" I said under my breath.

That wasn't a nice thing to say, and I immediately regretted even thinking it. Grandma did this every day. I had no right to complain.

Although I was tired beyond words, I hoped I was a help to Grandma, not a hindrance. I tried my best, and the job got a little easier as the day went on.

Thankfully, Mr. Martin never interfered with my work again. In fact, he never returned after he left with the old newspapers. I didn't know where he went, but it wasn't my job to keep track of him.

"Well, that's that for the day," Grandma said.

She locked the door, grabbed the café's ledger from under the lunch counter and walked over to where I was sitting. She looked as tired as I felt.

"Well, my dear," she said. "That was quite the first day of work for you."

That almost sounded like a compliment. At least it didn't sound like a complaint. I wasn't sure either way.

"It really was a long day, Grandma."

She walked to the front of the dining room and dropped the ledger on the front table. As usual, she passed by Grandpa's chair and sat down on a hard wooden one.

I got up, went over to her table and plopped down across from her the way I did that morning. I fought the urge to kick off my shoes.

For several minutes, Grandma shuffled through receipts, separating them into several piles in the middle of the table. She totaled each pile and jotted the number in a column in the ledger. Watching her was hypnotic, and I struggled to keep my eye lids from slamming shut.

"This is the job your grandfather did so well," she said, jolting me wide awake. "I never thought I would have to concern myself with such details."

Mom had told me about Grandpa's excellent business skills, but it looked to me as though Grandma was just as good. However, the longer I watched her work, the harder the chair got, and the more bored I became.

"There must be something I can do around here to help," I said.

Grandma stopped writing. She put the pen down beside the ledger and looked at me.

"There is something you can do."

She had my full attention. I hoped it was something to do with food because neither of us stopped to eat lunch.

"You can run across the street and pick up our supper at the general store."

Bingo. But wait a minute. We were in the café. Why go to the general store?

"Can't Irene fix something for us?"

"Irene has already cleaned up the kitchen and left for the day."

Things were getting interesting if not totally confusing. First, Mr. Martin disappeared. Then, Irene.

"Okay," I said. "When I get back we can walk home together."

"Not today," she said. "I don't want you coming back here."

"Why not?"

"I have a little more business to attend to."

"I don't mind waiting."

She looked at me with piercing eyes, and I knew what that meant. Stop arguing and do what you're told.

"Okay, Grandma. I'll meet you at home."

She dismissed me with a wave of her hand, picked up the pen and bent over the ledger again. The conversation was over.

I scooted my chair away from the table as quietly as possible, trying not to disturb her. I didn't understand why she didn't want me to wait for her, but I was glad to have a chance to visit with Aunt Maude. I plucked my sweater from its hook and left without a backward glance.

Traffic on Main Street was thinning out, and there was no longer a parade of people going in and out of the stores. Willowdale was definitely winding down for the day.

When I walked into the general store, I was met by a familiar sight. Aunt Maude, wearing a housedress and her hair braided across the top of her head, stood behind the mail counter and sorted letters into the mailboxes against the back wall. She was singing about someone called Barney Google.

"Who's Barney Google?"

I must have really startled her because she jumped a little before she turned around. When she saw me standing by the door, she dropped her handful of mail on the counter and smiled that wide smile I loved so much.

"Look what the cat dragged in."

"Hi, Aunt Maude," I said. "I came to pick up supper."

I hurried over to her and threw my arms around her neck. She squeezed me against her ample bosom in a long hug, rocking us both back and forth. Maybe I hated being hugged by someone I barely knew, but a hug from Aunt Maude was special. She was like family.

Just when I thought she would squeeze all the air out of me, she pushed me away and held me at arm's length. Her soft brown eyes studied my face.

"You've grown some since I saw you last."

Seeing the love for me written all over her face, it was easy to forget she wasn't my real aunt. Everyone in town called her Aunt Maude even though none of us was related to her.

"What's that wonderful smell?"

"Your grandma told me you'd be working today," she said. "I baked up a big batch of cookies last night for a meeting at the church this afternoon. I kept a few of them for you and your grandma."

She pulled out a plate of her famous chocolate chip cookies from under the counter. The plate was wrapped in red cellophane and tied with a white ribbon.

"They're a welcome back present from me to you."

"Thank you, Aunt Maude. I can hardly wait to try one."

"I don't see why you can't have one right now."

She dragged a plastic container from under the counter and set it in front of me. I removed the lid, studied the cookies and chose the largest one.

Before I had a chance to take the first bite, Jim barged through the door with two newspapers in his hand. He tossed them onto a small table beside the door.

"Here are your evening editions, Aunt Maude."

He was breathless, and his face was flushed. He stood by the door and shifted his weight from one foot to the other.

"Good gracious, Jimmy," she said. "What's your hurry?"

"I'd really like to visit, but I have to get home."

"You mean to tell me you don't have time to eat a cookie with me and Shirley?"

He pulled the baseball cap from his head, releasing a cascade of blonde curls. This time, he didn't bother to straighten his hair.

"Sorry. No time today."

He didn't stop fidgeting with his cap or stop shifting his weight. It was obvious to me he wanted to get out of there and fast.

"Here, now," Aunt Maude said. "I'll get you some cookies, and you can be on your way."

While she put a dozen or so of the cookies in a paper bag, Jim finally looked at me. He even smiled a little.

"Hi, Shirley."

"Hi, Jim."

Aunt Maude rolled down the top of the bag and stepped over to the cash register. She pushed the "no sale" lever and retrieved several coins from the drawer.

"Have you two young people already met?"

"Yes, ma'am."

"That's nice."

She went over to Jim and handed him the bag of cookies and the coins for the papers. Before he could turn to leave, she put her hand on his arm.

"Not even enough time to stop and visit with George?"

"Sorry, I can't."

"He's just taking a nap," she said. "He'll be real disappointed if you don't at least say hello."

"Sorry," he said. "But thanks for the cookies."

He dropped the coins in his pants pocket and jammed his cap back on his head. With a brief wave, he called to us over his shoulder as he ran outside.

"Bye, Aunt Maude. Bye, Shirley."

When the door closed behind him, Aunt Maude went back behind the counter. She sat down on a tall stool and shook her head.

"Poor boy," she said.

After all that, I realized I was still holding a cookie. I took a bite and wondered why Jim Spencer seemed to be everywhere I went and why he was always in such a hurry.

"What do you mean, Aunt Maude?"

She pulled a handkerchief from her dress pocket. After she mopped at perspiration streaking her forehead, she dabbed at small dots of perspiration lining her upper lip.

"Is it hot in here?" she said.

"No. Not really."

"Well, at any rate," she said, fanning her face with the handkerchief. "Jimmy delivers papers to the whole town every day on that rickety bicycle of his."

"Oh?"

"Now that he's out of school for the summer, he spends the rest of the day working for his father at the mill."

What good was summer vacation, I thought, if all you did was work?

"He must take some time off for fun."

"No, I don't think so," she said. "He's a hard worker."

"Well, it just doesn't seem right to work so hard on such a beautiful day."

"I suppose it doesn't."

I finished my cookie in four huge bites and reached for another one. Before I took the first bite of that one, I heard clicking sounds coming from Aunt Maude's apartment at the back of the store.

"Come on out, George," she said. "There's someone here to see you."

Her ten-year-old fawn pug waddled into the room. His toe nails clicked against the wooden floor, and his curly tail wagged so hard his whole rear end moved back and forth.

I put my cookie on the end of the counter and knelt down. With outstretched arms, I greeted Willowdale's littlest resident and unofficial mascot.

"Hello, George."

I took his head in my hands and gave him a kiss on the top of his wrinkled head. For a few seconds, he stopped wagging his tail and studied me. Then, he snorted in my face, and I knew he recognized me.

"I've missed you, big guy, but I can't stay long this time."

"Don't tell me you're in a hurry, too?"

"I'm afraid so, Aunt Maude. There's one more thing I want to do before I go home."

"Don't forget about your supper and your cookies."

"I won't."

I planted one last kiss on the top of George's head, stood up and grabbed my cookie off the end of the counter. Without a pause, I threw both of them a quick wave and rushed out the door.

"I'll be right back."

Seeing Aunt Maude and little George was just what I needed to perk me up. In fact, I felt so much better I almost forgot about my aching feet. Almost.

Ten

Liz's family had operated the flour mill for as long as I could remember. It seemed strange they were gone, and Jim's father owned it.

"Well," I said, walking as fast as my sore feet allowed. "Here's my chance to finally see the inside of it."

At the end of Main Street, I turned right at George's favorite fire hydrant and onto the gravel road leading to the mill. The rocks in the road were sharp against the thin soles of my dress flats, and they reminded me just how sore my feet really were. Instead of walking down the center of the road the way I used to do when I visited at Liz's house, I picked my way along the edge where new shoots of rye grass poked up between the rocks.

It took longer to walk to the mill than I remembered, and I was afraid Jim would be gone by the time I got there. But someone was inside. The barn door facing the top of the steep, dirt ramp was open wide enough to walk through, and dust as fine as mist seeped out of the opening.

"Jim?"

I stood just outside and listened to the sound of bristles scraping against wood. When he didn't answer, I ignored the dust and stepped through the door into the cool interior.

I could barely see Jim at the back of the dim, cavernous room. He was pushing a broom across the wooden floor and raising clouds of dust. He didn't stop until I walked over to him and shouted his name.

"Jim!"

He looked up at me for only a moment and then continued to sweep at the dirt and bits of grain. I waited while he finished sweeping it all into a single pile of debris.

"Can't you stop for just a minute?"

"Nope."

I glanced around the room. No one else was there.

"Where's your Dad?"

"He's not here."

"Where'd he go?"

Jim looked at me with a frown. I was probably being a little pushy.

"He went to a meeting."

"Well, anyway," I said. "I was hoping you'd give me a tour of this place."

"A tour?" he said. "I don't have time for any tour."

He turned his back to me and propped the broom against a wooden post. Without a word, he hurried past me to a set of narrow stairs and climbed up.

"Couldn't you take a little break?"

"I don't take breaks," he said and disappeared into the floor above.

I didn't know where the stairs led, but I followed after him anyway. When he didn't stop or look back at me, I was pretty sure he didn't know I was behind him.

The stairs led to a small room on the top floor that was ringed by windows on every wall. In spite of the jumble of belts and pulleys and wooden chutes in the center of the room, the light was brighter than downstairs. And there was no dust in the air.

When Jim saw me, he shook his head and said, "You're still here?"

I ignored him and looked around. The aged wood of the post and beam construction gave the room a pungent odor, and I fought back the impulse to hold my nose.

"I wanted to see the inside of a mill."

"You're telling me you've never been inside this place before?"

"Liz's father said mills are too dangerous for girls."

"Who's Liz?"

"This used to be her dad's mill."

"Well, he was right."

Jim stood with his fists on his hips. He wasn't smiling, but I didn't care. I went out of my way to get there on two very achy feet, and I wasn't about to take no for an answer.

"Just a little tour is all."

"No," he said. "I have to get done before Dad gets back from his meeting with your grandmother."

Grandma never told me about a meeting. I thought she was working on the café's ledger.

"What kind of meeting?"

He didn't answer. Instead, he pulled a stubby broom and a metal dustpan from two wooden pegs and swept around the belts and chutes. Whole pieces of grain and some chaff dropped to the floor.

While he worked, I went to one of the windows on the back wall. In the distance, I could clearly see Willow Creek meandering among a checkerboard of corn and wheat fields.

About a hundred feet away, an earthen dam diverted a small stream away from the main creek and directed it toward the mill. It was fascinating to watch the rippling water pass under the mill's wooden wheel, travel alongside the building's concrete foundation and flow back into the main creek.

"You must love coming up here," I said. "I don't think there's a more beautiful view anywhere else in Willowdale."

Jim didn't answer. He merely grunted at me and continued sweeping around the equipment.

I turned away from the window and watched him scoop debris off the floor with the dustpan, throw it all into a wooden barrel and begin to sweep again. The longer he swept, more and more dust rose and mingled with that filtering up from downstairs. I coughed and sneezed, then changed the subject.

"What do people do around this town for fun?"

"I don't know," he said.

"You must have some idea."

"I suppose some people play a little baseball or go fishing."

I groaned. That didn't sound like much fun to me.

"What do you like to do for fun?" I said.

He didn't answer me. He scooped up the last pile of debris, tossed it into the barrel with the rest and hung the broom and dustpan back on their pegs.

Without a word or any warning, he turned around and raced down the steps. I ran after him, but he was headed down to a lower level even before I reached the first floor.

"That's all the tour for today," he called from somewhere below me. "Go home."

"You don't need to be so rude."

I gasped for a breath of fresh air, but there wasn't any in the dense cloud of dust suspended throughout the room. My eyes burned and tears ran down my cheeks. I tried rubbing the burn away. That only made the tears flow faster, and it blurred my vision.

Disoriented, I stumbled through the first floor, searching for a way out. A dim light to my right revealed the small opening I entered only minutes before. I ran for it and bolted outside.

"Well, Grandma, you don't need to worry about Jim," I said loudly enough for Jim to hear. "He's the last person I want to be friends with."

I stood just outside the door and sucked in clean air. Even though I stopped rubbing my eyes, they still burned, and the tears still flowed down my face. To add to my misery, an involuntary fit of coughing struck me as my body tried to clear my lungs of the dust.

I wasn't the brightest person who ever lived, but I understood one thing. Liz's dad was right. The mill was no place for this girl.

Eleven

Marie Ivey stood beside the refreshment table and scanned the crowd seated on the folding chairs. Everyone there was a friend. She was sure she could count on their help.

When they finished eating the cookies her best friend, Maude, had baked, she stepped forward to start the meeting. The voices hushed when she began to speak.

"I want to thank all of you for coming here this afternoon."

"This better be important," Bill Spencer said. "I don't want to leave my boy alone at the mill for very long."

"That's right," said Harriet Spitz. "I told Julie she wouldn't have to cover for me for long. She vowed she'd never be a phone operator again, and I don't want to take advantage."

"The cows aren't going to milk themselves," Horace Wilson said.

There was some more grumbling until Aunt Maude stood up. She stepped to the front of the room and stood beside Marie.

"Now, listen here," she said, raising her hand for silence and eyeing anyone who was still complaining. "All of you know Marie wouldn't ask any of us here if it wasn't important."

"Then, get on with it," Horace said.

He twisted around in his chair and nodded at Mr. Martin standing at the back of the room. Most everyone mumbled in agreement.

"Thank you, Maude," Marie said. "And thank you for the wonderful cookies."

When the room was completely quiet, Marie took a folded piece of paper from her pocket. She stole a quick glance at it and put it on the table.

"The Fourth of July isn't very far away," she said. "And it's going to be Shirley's sixteenth birthday."

"What's that got to do with us?"

"Well, Bill, I want to throw her a surprise party, and I need all of you to help."

"Oh, yeah?" he said. "What kind of help?"

Marie walked around to the front of the table and took a deep breath. She brushed at imaginary wrinkles in the skirt of her dress and cleared her throat.

"I thought it could be a potluck dinner in the high school gym," she said. "No presents, of course, but I will need a birthday cake."

"A birthday cake?" someone at the back of the room said.

"And there will be fireworks afterward."

"Fireworks!"

There were so many people shouting at her, she stopped talking. Her hands shook, and she strained to keep her composure.

Finally, Mr. Martin went forward and banged on the table with one of the coffee cups. He kept banging until the room was quiet again.

"Stop yer bellyachin'," he said. "Let her have her say."

All those who had stood up, sat down. All those who had been talking, glared at him.

"I spoke with Bob McNary, the president of the Monticello chapter of the Central Indiana Men's Association," she said. "My Robert was a charter member, and they want to honor his memory by showcasing their Fourth of July fireworks in Willowdale this year.

"What about the article ya wrote?"

"That's right, Mr. Martin," she said. "I've already put an article in the newspaper and invited the whole county to come."

"Okay," Bill said. "But that doesn't explain the party."

"Yeah, I'm with you," Horace said, standing up again. "None of us can afford to throw parties for our own kids."

Marie knew almost everyone there had children, but she wasn't deterred. She was determined to make the party work for her granddaughter.

"Don't we always have our annual Willowdale social that day anyway?" she said. "And don't we usually have it potluck?"

"We do," Harriet said as the people around her nodded their heads in agreement.

"I propose we combine a party for Shirley with our annual potluck and invite the members of Bob's chapter and their families to come," Marie said. "We'll bring all our favorite dishes to share as usual, and afterward, we'll watch the fireworks with the whole county."

Bill sat up straighter and nodded to the person next to him. His eyes were bright with excitement.

"I think that just might work," he said. "Jimmy and I can get all the church's folding tables and chairs to the gym in the back of my truck."

"I would be honored to bring the birthday cake," Aunt Maude said.

As each one volunteered to cover a part of the arrangements, Marie wrote down each offer on the piece of paper on the table. She was overwhelmed by their generosity. After such a rocky start, the meeting turned out better than she had hoped.

"I can't thank all of you enough," she said. "Ivey's Café will be donating hot dogs and buns."

Marie was still writing notes until Mr. Martin stood up again. He didn't need to bang on the table with a cup. The noise in the room stopped immediately.

"That's all settled," he said, tossing his hat on the seat of his chair. "Let's clean this place up an' git on home."

Twelve

I swung back and forth on the wooden swing in Grandma's back yard, rested my head against the backrest and let the soft breeze cool my face. Each time the swing moved, the two ropes suspending it from an overhead limb rubbed against the bark and protested with a loud creak.

When I was only a little girl, Grandpa removed the swing from the front porch. He painted it a bright yellow and hung it from the tree for me.

"If you ever need somewhere to relax and unwind," he had said, "this is the perfect place."

Grandpa was right. I needed its gentle, calming motion.

"What a day."

Thanks to Jim's rudeness, my trip to the old mill didn't take very long, and when I got back to the general store, Aunt Maude was closing up early. She had our supper and cookies ready for me, so I got home with our food before Grandma.

"All I wanted was a tour," I said. "Guess that was just too much to ask."

My feet throbbed from walking all day in my dress flats, and every muscle in my body screamed from exhaustion. I found it hard to understand why Grandma wanted to work so hard at her age.

I looked down at my feet and studied my swollen ankles. The only positive thing about my situation was my pair of well-worn moccasins. I put them on when I got home, and they felt soft against my skin.

"From now on, it's socks and saddle oxfords at work."

As I contemplated the wisdom of throwing away my dress flats, I sniffed the air and smelled supper on the stove. My stomach growled.

Following Aunt Maude's detailed instructions, I put the pot of stew on the stove to keep it warm and put the plate of cookies on the dining room table. Grandma and I were definitely going to eat well.

It's so ironic, I thought. Grandma owns a café, and she can't cook.

"Oh, well. As long as Irene is there, everything will be fine."

I pulled my legs up under me and closed my eyes. The back and forth motion of the swing threatened to lull me to sleep. Not even the chatter of a squirrel in the oak tree next to the garage disturbed me.

I rubbed my hand over my empty stomach. It growled again.

Come on, Grandma, I thought. I'm starving.

"Shirley?"

My eyes popped open. Grandma appeared from around the corner of the garage, high-stepping through the thick lawn. She was grinning, and her cheeks were flushed.

"Grandma, are you alright?"

Her grin widened into a smile the closer she came. In her hands she clutched a bundle of orange day lilies, purple bachelor buttons and some greenery I didn't recognize.

"I just couldn't resist," she said. "Aren't they beautiful?"

Several strands of her hair hung from the bun at her neck. The lace collar on her dress was unbuttoned, and the toes of her work shoes were scuffed.

"Are you sure you're okay?"

As she got even closer, I could hear her labored breathing. That didn't sound good. I jumped off the swing and started toward her.

"I decided to come home through the cornfield," she said. "As it turns out, the edges of the field are covered with wildflowers right now."

She giggled like a young girl, and I had to laugh at her. I couldn't imagine what happened to make her so happy since I saw her at the café.

I stepped up onto the porch and followed her into the house. She dropped the flowers on the counter next to the sink, and I walked beside her while she circled the perimeter of the kitchen. She opened and closed every cabinet as she went.

"I know it's here somewhere," she said.

"What are you looking for, Grandma?"

At the last cabinet, she paused. Several vases were huddled together on the top shelf.

"Aha."

"Aha?"

"There," she said. "Would you mind handing that one to me?"

I stretched up on my tiptoes and pulled down a white porcelain vase. All around its grazed surface were painted gaudy red roses.

"There're so many other prettier ones to choose from, Grandma."

She took the vase from me and hugged it to her chest. Tears filled her eyes when she looked at me again.

"This one came with the first bouquet your grandfather ever gave me."

"I just thought another one might look better with those particular flowers."

"No," she said, waving her hand in my direction. "This one is perfect."

She filled the vase with water, arranged the flowers in it and carried the bouquet into the dining room. When she placed the flowers in the center of the table, I moved the plate of cookies to the buffet.

We both stood back a step to admire the arrangement, and I realized she was right. The bouquet was beautiful, and the vase was perfect.

Thirteen

"Sure was a long day, Mrs. Ivey," Mr. Martin said to himself. "Startin' with me callin' up all those nice folks ta meet ya at the church."

He started the engine in the old truck, turned on the headlights and fumbled with the gear shift. The transmission groaned in protest, so he stepped on the clutch pedal twice and forced it into reverse. Slowly, he backed away from the Sunday school entrance.

"Ya sure did ruffle some feathers when ya talked about havin' fireworks," he said. "I figured there'd be a fight right there in the meetin' room."

Now that everybody knew the whole story, their reaction seemed pretty funny to him. But at the time, he understood why all of them were so upset. They couldn't afford to spoil their children the way Mrs. Ivey wanted to spoil Shirley.

"City kids," he said. "They never had ta live simple like countryfolk."

He pulled the truck out of the church's parking lot, turned left onto 2nd Street and drove straight ahead. When the street dead ended at Main Street, he slammed on the breaks and threw the gear shift into neutral.

Up and down the street, the stores were closed for the day, and there wasn't a light on in any of them. All of them except for Aunt Maude's general store.

"Would ya look at that?"

All the overhead lights were on, illuminating the interior of her store with an eerie yellow glow. He expected to see Aunt Maude through the huge front window, but there wasn't any movement inside.

"Ya oughta be home from the meetin' by now," he said. "Why's yer store still all lit up?"

For several seconds, he waited for someone to go in or out of the store. But there was no one in sight anywhere on Main Street.

"I bet ya just fergot ta turn 'em out."

He was tired from all the chores Mrs. Ivey had him do all day. The last thing he wanted to do was worry about Aunt Maude's lights.

He didn't even want to think about tomorrow. But after the meeting, Mrs. Ivey handed him a long list of things to buy in Monticello for the surprise potluck.

"If I'm gonna git up early ta drive ta the city, I gotta git some sleep."

He held the shift lever in a tight grip and forced the transmission into first gear. He gave the general store one last look, turned onto Main Street and pointed the truck toward home.

The streetlights and the light on the water tower were already on, but they weren't bright enough for him. He turned on the truck's bright lights and stared at the road ahead.

"Can't hardly see a thing," he said. "Guess these old eyes aren't what they used ta be."

On the edge of town, he didn't see where the pavement ended, and he drove onto the gravel without slowing down. The truck's front tire caught the edge of a pothole, and the empty bottles on the seat next to him clanked together. He reached over and steadied the crates.

"Whoa there," he said. "Can't be breakin' any bottles."

He slowed his speed a little more, squinted at the road ahead and leaned closer to the windshield. It was hard enough for him to drive in town where there were a few streetlights, but outside of town there was nothing to help guide him. So, with one hand on the crates and steering with the other, he aimed the truck down the center of the deserted road.

"Sure glad I got them old papers outa the café," he said. "It woulda spoilt the surprise if Shirley read how her grandma invited all them folks ta see the fireworks."

Fourteen

We were nearly finished eating when the phone in the kitchen rang. I started to get up to go answer it, but Grandma shook her head and dabbed at the corners of her mouth with her napkin.

"No, dear, you enjoy your supper," she said. "I'll answer the phone."

Aunt Maude's stew was delicious, and I was only too happy to stay there and finish. The gaudy vase in the center of the table and the beautiful wildflowers made the meal even more special.

After only a minute or two, Grandma came back to the dining room. I wanted to tell her what a good time I was having at supper, but she looked upset. Her smile was gone, and she began pacing from the dining table to the buffet and back.

"Grandma, what's wrong?"

"I'm sure it's nothing," she said. "Maude has a tendency to overreact."

"Overreact about what?"

"I'm not quite sure," she said. "She seems a bit upset and wants to see me."

"You mean she wants to see you right now?"

"I'm afraid so."

I didn't need any more explanation than that. I jumped up from the table and gathered up the dirty dishes. While Grandma disappeared into her bedroom, I carried everything to the kitchen.

I looked down at my moccasins. Their soft soles felt good on my aching feet, but they were no match for a walk to town on the gravel road. It only took me a couple of minutes to run upstairs and exchange them for my socks and saddle oxfords.

I hopped down the stairs two steps at a time and arrived at the landing just as Grandma opened her bedroom door. Her hair was pinned neatly into place, her dress was straightened and her shoes were buffed clean.

"I'm certain I won't be very long."

She hurried toward the kitchen. Before she reached the back door, I ran ahead of her and blocked the way. I grabbed our sweaters from their hooks and handed one to her.

"I'm coming, too."

"There's really no need for both of us to go."

"Haven't you always told me a woman should never walk alone at night?"

"I'll be fine," she said. "This is just Willowdale."

"I know."

Not waiting for more of her excuses, I picked up the flashlight from the table, hooked my arm around Grandma's elbow and led her outside. She was trembling and a little unsteady.

Before I switched on the flashlight, it looked as though a million lightning bugs blinked on and off among the lilac bushes along the side of the porch. The Milky Way and all the other stars were brilliant against the night sky, and somewhere in the distance, an owl hooted.

"It's just too nice tonight for anything to be wrong with her, Grandma."

"I certainly hope you're right, dear."

I didn't know if I tried to convince Grandma or myself nothing bad could happen on such a gorgeous night. But I was pretty sure keeping a positive attitude didn't hurt.

Using the flashlight to guide us, we walked the rest of the way in silence until we reached the general store. The front door was unlocked, and all the overhead lights were on. When Grandma eased the door open about a foot or so, George began yipping from inside Aunt Maude's apartment.

"Maude?" Grandma said. "Are you here?"

Not waiting for a response, we went inside, closed the door behind us and hurried to the rear of the store. Light spilled from under the apartment door.

"Maude," Grandma said and knocked on the door as hard as she could.

I stood directly behind her. We both listened for an answer, but George yipped incessantly on the other side of the door. He made it impossible to hear anything else.

"Maude, I'm coming in."

When Grandma stepped inside the apartment, the little pug squeezed past her and escaped into the store. He bumped up against my leg, and I picked him up.

His tail wagged, and his whole body shook. When I gave him a hug, he turned his head toward me and slathered my face with kisses.

"Oh, George."

"Shirley," Grandma said from inside the apartment. "I need you to call Dr. Thompson."

"Dr. Thompson?" I said. "Really?"

"Just do what I ask, young lady, and don't ask questions."

"Yes, Grandma."

I put George down, wiped my wet face on the sleeve of my sweater and ran to the wall telephone under the sign that read "Post Office". My hands shook almost as badly as George, and I took a deep breath to try to calm my nerves.

When the operator came on the line, I asked her to ring Dr. Thompson. I didn't bother to give an explanation.

"Shirley, is that you?"

"Yes, it is."

"Your grandmother told me you were visiting," she said. "Is everything alright?"

"Grandma and I are at the general store."

"Yes, I can see that."

Of course, I thought. She can see Aunt Maude's number on the switchboard.

"Grandma and I are fine."

I swallowed hard and took another deep breath. Even so, my voice cracked when I spoke.

"It's Aunt Maude," I said. "Grandma says she needs a doctor."

"Don't worry," she said. "I'll ring Dr. Thompson's house right now and let him know."

"Thanks."

My hands trembled as I replaced the receiver. When I looked down, George was standing at my feet and staring up at me with his wide, brown eyes.

"Come on, big guy," I said. "Let's go tell Grandma and Aunt Maude the doctor is on his way."

The little pug padded after me into the apartment. I found Grandma in the bedroom, sitting on the edge of the bed and fanning Aunt Maude's face with the issue of a fashion magazine.

"I'm sure it's nothing," Grandma said.

"But you know my brother has a bad heart."

"Yes, yes, I know."

Grandma spoke softly while she waved the magazine back and forth. I could see from the look in her eyes how concerned she was for her friend.

As haggard looking as Grandma was after her long day at the café, Aunt Maude looked even worse. Her face was as pale as the white sheets on her bed, and a line of perspiration dotted her upper lip.

"Dr. Thompson will be here soon," Grandma said. "Isn't that right, Shirley?"

I tried to sound calm. I didn't want either of them to worry about anything else, but my voice was as shaky as my hands.

"That's right, Grandma."

George waddled across the room, his toe nails clicking. When he reached the bed, he stood up on his hind legs and rested his front paws on the edge of the mattress.

"I'll be alright, George," Aunt Maude said.

While she stroked the top of his head, the front door clicked open, then shut with a bang. I stepped into the store and found Dr. Thompson standing in the center of the room clutching a black leather bag.

"She's in here," I said and motioned for him to follow me.

Once inside the bedroom, the doctor immediately went over to Aunt Maude. He dropped his medical bag on the floor, snapped open the clasp and pulled out a stethoscope.

"Well, now," he said. "I understand you aren't feeling very well."

In order to allow them privacy, Grandma and I left the apartment and waited in the store. George stayed in the bedroom with Aunt Maude.

While we waited for Dr. Thompson to finish his examination, I was too nervous to stand still. I paced around the store and read labels on canned goods and the backs of cereal boxes. Grandma, on the other hand, sat unusually quiet on the tall stool behind the counter.

"Why are you so calm, Grandma?"

"I've learned to be patient where Maude is concerned," she said. "Very seldom is anything really wrong with her."

"I hope you're right this time."

I continued to pace for what seemed like hours. But the clock behind the counter said it was only a few minutes before

Dr. Thompson came out to talk to us. He carried his leather bag at his side, and George followed closely behind him.

"I'm taking Aunt Maude into Lafayette to the hospital, Mrs. Ivey."

"Is that really necessary?"

"It appears she has a rather significant heart irregularity," he said. "And she's complaining of back pain and hot spells."

"Ye gods," Grandma said. "Are those things significant?"

"I can't make a definitive diagnosis here, but they could be very significant."

"I'll go help her pack an overnight case."

When Grandma was inside the apartment and out of hearing range, the doctor looked over at me. His face was somber, and he barely spoke above a whisper.

"Aunt Maude would like you and Jimmy to watch after George while she's gone."

"Gee whiz," I said. "I don't know."

"I told her it might be too much of an imposition."

"Oh, no, it isn't that at all. I just don't know how Grandma would feel about it."

"How I would feel about what?"

Grandma appeared in the apartment doorway. She held a small overnight case in one hand and Aunt Maude's purse in the other.

"She needs someone to care for George, Mrs. Ivey," he said.

The little pug brushed past me and shuffled over to Grandma. As if he understood what was at stake, he sat down and stared up at her. I stood behind him with my lip pushed outward.

"He's a very nice little dog," I said. "I promise to feed him and walk him every day."

I didn't know which would work better to convince Grandma. Would it be my silly pout or George's irresistible face?

Grandma dropped the overnight case and the purse on the floor and knelt down in front of George. When he lifted a chubby paw to her bent knee, she smiled.

"You little minx," she said. "It looks as though you'll be spending a little time with us."

"You mean it, Grandma?"

"If you think you're up to the task of caring for him."

"I promise you I am."

"Then, he'll be going home with us tonight."

"Oh, thank you, Grandma," I said. "I'll take really good care of him."

"I know you will, dear."

Dr. Thompson eased past Grandma and George, went inside the apartment and closed the door. The little pug didn't budge. He continued to stare at Grandma, cocking his head back and forth. She had his full attention until the apartment door swung open again.

"Here they come," I said.

Grandma stood up, and George padded over to Aunt Maude. I couldn't help but smile a little at him as I picked up her overnight case and purse.

"Don't worry about a thing, Maude," Grandma said. "Everything will be just fine."

Aunt Maude didn't answer her or even look at George. She just leaned against Dr. Thompson, and they walked out of the store.

While the doctor settled her into the front seat of his car, I trailed after them with a little bounce in my step. I put the overnight case and her purse on the back seat.

"Don't worry about George, Aunt Maude," I said. "I'll take really good care of him."

"I'm counting on you and Jimmy to do just that," she said. "And tell your grandmother I'm sorry about spoiling her plans."

I placed my hand on her shoulder. She felt warm under my touch, and rivulets of perspiration trickled down her face. The same way she looked when I saw her in the store that afternoon.

"I'll tell her, Aunt Maude."

When Dr. Thompson started his car's engine, I raced back inside the store and stood at the front window beside Grandma. George bumped up against me again, and I scooped him into my arms.

This is going to be neat, I thought. It'll be almost like having my own dog.

"I almost forgot, Grandma," I said. "Aunt Maude wanted me to tell you she's sorry about spoiling your plans."

"Oh?"

The three of us watched the car slip away into the night. I moved George's paw up and down in a waving motion.

"What plans, Grandma?"

"They're nothing for you to be concerned about."

I couldn't tell by her expression whether she was concerned about the plans Aunt Maude talked about or not. I did know she was concerned about her best friend. We all were.

Fifteen

Instead of going around to the back, Mr. Martin parked the old truck outside the café's front door. It was an hour before Mrs. Ivey and Shirley would arrive for the day, and he was pretty sure he wouldn't get caught.

First thing that morning, he had called everyone who was at Mrs. Ivey's meeting at the church. Most of them said it was too early for him to be calling, and he knew it. But once he explained how urgent it was, some of them agreed to meet with him.

"Anyways, it'll be quick," he told them.

Because none of the stores was open that early, Main Street was completely abandoned except for one other person. At the end of the street, Jimmy sat on the curb in front of the bank. He was rolling up newspapers and stuffing them into the saddlebags on the back of his bike.

"He's a good boy, that one."

He eased out of the truck and stepped up onto the sidewalk. Pulling at the ring of keys dangling from his belt, he fumbled with them until he found the key to the café.

"Too bad about Aunt Maude," he said to himself. "She's a good ol' gal, an' she oughta be here ta help."

When Mrs. Ivey called to tell him Aunt Maude was in the hospital, she said she wanted to change the plans for the potluck. If Aunt Maude couldn't be there, she wanted to call the whole thing off.

"That'd be a down right shame," he said. "An' Aunt Maude wouldn't take kindly ta cancelin' it."

As he fit the key into the lock, a truck loaded with bales of straw passed by, and he waved at the young driver. Then, a faded green Chevy sedan pulled into a diagonal parking space directly across the street. Harriet, the town's telephone operator, was in the front seat.

"Good," he said. "Ya sure can count on Harriet ta be early."

With Aunt Maude so sick, Mrs. Ivey wanted him to cancel his trip into Monticello for the Fourth of July supplies. She didn't even want him to go get milk, but he couldn't see the sense in any of that. The café needed milk, and everybody looked forward to the potluck. He decided he would figure out a way to pay for the supplies with his own money if he had to.

"Nope," he said. "I sure don't see a reason fer cancelin' our plans."

He unlocked the door and went inside. Leaving the door ajar, he went straight to the kitchen, poured water and ground coffee into the percolator and turned on the gas burner underneath it.

"If we do this right, it'll be the best potluck this town's ever had."

When the percolator was finished, he carried the pot and several cups into the dining room. Harriet was already sitting at one of the tables, and he saw the drawn look on her face.

"This better be important," she said. "I have to go to work in a few minutes."

"It's important alright," he said and placed the cups on the table.

He settled down on one of the chairs across from her and poured coffee into two of the cups. He slid one of them in front of her.

"Hmm," she said.

She grabbed the cup and blew across the surface of the hot liquid. The rising steam fogged the lenses of her horn-rimmed glasses.

Before he could ask how she was feeling, Bill Spencer and Clyde, Horace Wilson's oldest boy, pushed through the front door. Without a word, they plopped themselves down on the remaining two chairs.

"Mornin' boys," he said. "How's it goin'?"

Each of the men grabbed an empty cup and poured himself some coffee. Neither of them spoke. They just stared at him and nursed their drinks.

"Mrs. Ivey wants ta cancel the surprise potluck," he said. "That'd be a shame, don't ya think?"

"If that don't beat all," Clyde said. "What's that you say?"

"You mean you got us here this morning to talk about the potluck?" Bill said.

He blew on his coffee and waited for Harriet to chime in. But she stayed as quiet as before, sipping her coffee between yawns.

"Mrs. Ivey thinks we'd be okay with her cancelin' everything 'cause of Aunt Maude bein' sick an' all."

"Yeah, so?" Clyde said.

"I'm with him," Bill said. "I don't see the problem."

"Well, I'm thinkin' Aunt Maude wouldn't want that," he said. "I'm thinkin' nobody else would either."

Harriet sat up straight and put her coffee cup on the table. She smoothed down some flyaway hair above her forehead and cleared her throat. The men stopped drinking their coffee and looked at her.

"You're right, Mr. Martin," she said. "Aunt Maude would love a good potluck, and she wouldn't want us to cancel ours."

"Yeah, well, she ain't here."

"Well, Clyde," she said. "It seems to me that having something to look forward to, whether she can be here or not, would be a real boost to her morale."

The three men sat quietly and looked at her. Mr. Martin hadn't even given that angle a thought, but he thought it was a good one.

"I'm thinkin' it'd be fun if we let Mrs. Ivey keep on thinkin' the whole thing's off," he said. "Make it a surprise fer both her an' Shirley."

Clyde and Bill stared at him for a few seconds. He waited while they poured themselves another cup of coffee.

"A double surprise," Bill said. "And we'd still have the fireworks?"

"I'm drivin' over ta Monticello tomorrow fer the supplies," he said. "I'll get hold of somebody over there ta make sure of it."

"Well, I'll be," Clyde said. "If the fireworks are still part of the deal, then I say let's go for it."

They all sat quietly and sipped their coffee until Harriet pushed her chair away from the table and jumped up. She pointed at her watch.

"I have to get to work," she said, heading toward the door. "What about Aunt Maude?"

"I'm drivin' over ta Lafayette today ta check on her."

"We don't have much time to get ready," Bill said. "And we don't want her spoiling the surprise."

"Don't ya worry," he said. "I'll tell her it's a double surprise so she don't spill the beans ta Mrs. Ivey."

"That takes care of Aunt Maude, but what about Marie?" Harriet said.

"Well, she's gonna think we're okay with her cancelin' everything," he said. "We'll just let her go ahead an' think it."

He put his cup down on the table and leaned back in his chair. They were counting on him, and he didn't want to disappoint anyone.

"If we tell all the folks ta keep the plans hush, hush," he said, "we'll have ourselves a double surprise potluck, fer sure."

"Don't you be forgittin' the fireworks, now," Clyde said. "That's the most important part."

"I'm not fergittin' the fireworks," he said. "It's the first thing I'm checkin' on tomorrow."

Sixteen

I opened one eye. A beam of sunlight from the dormer window fell across my face, and I basked in its warmth. The room seemed especially cozy, and I didn't want to get out of bed.

Finally, I forced myself to open both of my eyes. When my bleary vision cleared enough, I rolled over and focused on the alarm clock. It read seven o'clock.

"Oh, no."

I jumped out of bed and grabbed the clock. I studied the hands on its face, hoping I misread them. I didn't.

"How could I over sleep?"

I checked the alarm button. It was turned off.

"I don't remember turning it off."

There was no time to think about that. I slammed the clock down on the nightstand, grabbed the afghan from the foot of the bed and threw it around my shoulders.

Not stopping for my slippers, I darted from the room. My bare feet thudded against the wooden floor as I raced down the hallway.

"Grandma, I'm so sorry I'm late."

I hopped down the steps, two at a time, with a loose corner of the afghan bouncing along behind me. At the bottom of the stairs, I stopped and sniffed the air.

There should have been the smell of coffee, but there was nothing. Not even burned toast, and the house was oddly quiet. The only sound was a faint whimpering coming from the kitchen.

"Coming, big guy."

At the sound of my voice, the whimpering stopped. By the time I reached the kitchen, George was sitting quietly and peering at me from behind the makeshift, cardboard enclosure I built for him. His blanket was rumpled, and his water bowl was empty.

"Oh, no," I said. "I promised Aunt Maude I'd take good care of you."

I pulled back one of the cardboard sides, and George walked over to me, wagging so hard his whole rear end moved back and forth. I knelt down and folded him inside the afghan with me, and he thanked me by licking my face.

"I know Grandma doesn't want dog hair all over the house, but Aunt Maude wouldn't want you to be penned in all the time."

When I released him from the warmth of the afghan, he turned away from me and walked over to the kitchen table. A bag of dog food sat in the center of it, and next to the bag was a note from Grandma. As I read it, George sat at my feet, panting.

"Well, big guy, Grandma had to leave early this morning."

I dropped the note in the garbage and retrieved two dog bowls from the floor. One I filled with water. The other I filled with George's morning ration of food.

"You eat up, now," I said. "I have to get dressed and get to work."

I didn't need to tell George what to do. Before I reached the kitchen door, he finished the kibble and licked the bowl clean.

Seventeen

Once I was dressed and back in the kitchen, I found George inside the enclosure again. His head was resting half on, half off the edge of the blanket, and his big, round eyes followed my every move as I wandered around the room looking for something to use as a leash.

I finally found a short length of clothesline in one of the cabinet drawers, and it only took a couple of minutes to tie a loop at each end of the cotton line. Although I could have stopped right then to fix myself some breakfast, I didn't want to waste any more time.

I grabbed my sweater off the hook by the back door and slipped it on. I secured one of the loops in the clothesline around George's collar and slid the other loop around my wrist. It took a little coaxing, but George finally got up and followed me outside.

I was in a rush to get to the café. I didn't want Grandma mad at me for oversleeping, but the little pug made it impossible to hurry. He plodded along, his paws flopping one after the other.

"George," I said. "At this rate, it'll take us a year to get to town."

As slowly as I walked, his tongue still hung from his mouth and his chest still heaved with each breath. I forced myself to slow down even more.

When we finally reached the county road at the end of the driveway, George stopped. He planted his feet in a bulldog stance and refused to budge.

I tried pulling on the leash to get him to move, but he continued to refuse. There was no choice but to pick him up and carry him.

I wrapped my arms around him and held him close to my chest. With the added weight, I couldn't walk as fast as I normally would, and after a few minutes, I was gasping for air myself. I wished a passing truck would offer us a ride. None did.

"Don't they realize we could use some help, big guy?"

George seemed unconcerned about the whole situation. The longer I walked, the more relaxed he became and the heavier he seemed to get.

"It's time for you to go on a diet, don't you think?"

When we got to the sidewalk on the edge of town, I put him down. My arms and my back ached, and I was on the verge of tears. I tried my hardest to be angry with him, but it was impossible when he cocked his head at me and wagged his tail.

"I know you're cute, but from here on, you're walking on your own four feet."

The smooth surface of the walk seemed to invigorate him, and he pulled against the leash. When we got to Main Street, he practically dragged me up the sidewalk toward the café.

I could see Grandma at the front door, smiling and waving at us. Behind her, several customers filed in and out, and all of them waved at us, too.

"I can't believe it, George. I don't think she's upset with us for being so late."

We were within yards of the café when Jim pedaled up to the front door and skidded to a halt. He took a bundle of newspapers out of one of the saddlebags and rushed up to Grandma.

"Morning, Mrs. Ivey."

"Good morning, Jimmy."

She opened the door for him and held it until he was inside. I was surprised she stayed outside and waited for us.

By the time George pulled me the rest of the way up the sidewalk, I was breathing normally again. It was easier without carrying him, but my wrist was sore from him constantly tugging on the leash.

"I hope you were able to get some extra rest this morning," Grandma said.

"I'm really sorry I'm late. The alarm didn't go off for some reason."

"Yes, I know," she said. "I turned it off this morning while you were asleep."

My mouth dropped open. Grandma allowed me to over-sleep?

"And it took George and me a little longer to get here than I thought it would."

George's corkscrew tale wagged back and forth, and he leaned up against Grandma's leg. It was obvious to me what he was doing. He was trying to charm Grandma, and it worked.

"That's alright this one time," she said, smiling down at the little pug. "You both needed your rest this morning since neither of you got much rest last night."

"What do you mean, Grandma?"

"Don't play innocent with me, young lady," she said. "You were up and down all night checking on George."

I felt my face turn red, and I was speechless. I thought I was as quiet as a mouse going up and down the stairs.

"Now, it's time to get to work," she said.

Before I had a chance to go inside, Jim came out of the café. He didn't bother to say hello to me. Instead, he knelt down and scratched the little dog behind his ears.

"Good morning, George."

"Well, young man," Grandma said. "Are you finished with the papers?"

"Yes, ma'am," he said. "I put all the new papers on the stand and piled the old ones on the floor."

"Good."

He stood up and brushed at some loose dog hair on his pants. When he finished, Grandma pulled several coins from her apron pocket and handed them to him.

"Just one more thing," she said. "I would like you to watch George today."

My mouth dropped open again. I knew Aunt Maude wanted both of us to take care of him, but this was his first day without her. I wanted to be the one to watch him.

"But, Grandma," I said, trying out my pouting lip routine. "I don't think George would mind spending the day watching me work."

"I'm sure he wouldn't," she said, her chin jutted upward. "But my café is no place for a dog."

It was clear my pout didn't impress either Grandma or Jim. He ignored me again, knelt beside George and gave him a big hug.

"You and I get to spend the day together," he said.

Reluctantly, I slipped the leash from my wrist and dropped it on the sidewalk. I wasn't going to give him the satisfaction of handing it to him.

"I'll come back later for my bike, Mrs. Ivey," he said, ruffing up George's thick mane.

I stood my ground and hovered over the little dog. I wanted to do something or say something to keep Jim from taking him away all day, but I couldn't. Grandma was right. No dog belonged in the café.

"So, where are you taking him?" I said.

"I'm watching the store for Aunt Maude today," he said. "He can spend the whole day sleeping on his own bed."

He snatched the leash and stood up. But before he had a chance to take even one step toward the general store, Grandma stepped forward. Her hands rested on her hips.

"Young man," she said. "Did your father ask you to do that?"

"No, ma'am, I just thought Aunt Maude would appreciate the help."

Grandma took another step forward. This time, she put her hands over her eyes to block the morning sun.

"That's very thoughtful of you, and I'd like to do something to thank you in return."

"You would?"

"You would?" I said.

"I would like it very much if you would join Shirley and me for lunch."

"Ma'am?"

"Grandma?"

I couldn't believe my ears. Grandma warned me not to think about boys, and she was inviting Jim to eat with us.

"Be here promptly at two o'clock."

"Ma'am?"

"Grandma?"

"Two o'clock, not a minute later."

"Yes, ma'am," he said, wearing his irritating grin. "See you then."

Grandma and I stood on the edge of the walk and watched him cross the street with George. A moment after they disappeared inside the general store, the "closed" sign in the window flipped to the "open" side.

"I don't understand, Grandma," I said. "Why did you invite him to lunch?"

She turned to me and scowled. This time her fists were jammed into her waist. Obviously, I spoke out of turn.

"Listen to me," she said. "A person should always be rewarded for doing something thoughtful without being asked."

I figured she was trying to tell me something, but I didn't have time to figure it out. My mind was too busy thinking about lunch.

While I stood there worrying about eating with someone I didn't particularly like, Grandma dug into the pocket of her apron. She pulled out a slip of paper and handed it to me with a flourish.

"Here are your errands for the day."

I took the note and read down the list. There were enough items on it to keep me busy at least all day, if not all week.

"But before you get started," she said. "Take the bike over to the general store for Jim."

"What?"

"We all have to do our part."

I shoved the list into the pocket of my blouse. Could this day get any worse? First, I was forced to leave George with Jim. Then, I was expected to help him by hauling his bike across the street.

"Right now, young lady."

It might have made me feel better to argue with her about the inconvenience it would cause me, but I was raised better than that. I had no choice in the matter, and there was no use stalling.

"Yes, Grandma."

"Be back here promptly at two o'clock."

"Yes, Grandma."

Eighteen

I walked the bike across the street and leaned it up against the front wall of the general store. Since Jim already delivered the newspapers, the bike's saddlebags weren't bulging. Even so, I wanted to make sure it was far enough to the side of the walk so Aunt Maude's customers wouldn't trip over it.

"It just isn't fair," I said. "Jim gets to watch George all day, and I have to traipse all over the countryside running errands for Grandma."

The longer I thought about it, the angrier I got. It wasn't bad enough to be forced to spend the whole summer working instead of having fun with my friends at home. I was forced to deal with Jim and his bike, too.

"Well, Jim, I have news for you," I said to myself. "I'm going to check on George before I start my errands whether you like it or not."

I eased the front door open, and watched for George. I was afraid he might get past me and wander into the street. That wouldn't be a good way to start my babysitting responsibilities, but I didn't need to worry. He was nowhere in sight, and neither was Jim.

"George," I said. "Where are you?"

I didn't hear any sounds coming from Aunt Maude's apartment or from anywhere inside the store. I knew neither of them could simply disappear.

"I came to say goodbye, George."

I closed the door and started toward the apartment. If Jim was irresponsible enough to leave the little pug alone, or worse, loose him, he was going to have to deal with me and my grandmother.

"Hi, Shirley, I'll be down in a second."

"What?"

Jim's voice was muffled, and I looked all around the store to see where it came from. It didn't take long to spot him on top of a tall, wooden ladder at the back of the room. He was teetering on the top rung.

"What in the world are you doing up there?"

A cardboard box of canned goods perched on the edge of the shelf in front of him. With an even rhythm, he pulled a can of baked beans from the box with one hand, stacked it on the shelf with the other hand and reached for another can without hesitating between moves.

I stood there for several seconds, fascinated. But then, I couldn't stand not saying something.

"How many times have you dropped a can?"

"Not many."

"Was anybody standing beside the ladder at the time?"

"Don't think so."

He flashed that annoying smile at me and dropped the empty box on the floor. Before I could think of something else to say, he propelled himself down the ladder and landed with a thud.

"Hi," he said. "I didn't think I'd see you again so soon."

"What's the matter with you?" I said.

"What do you mean?"

"What I mean is, you coming down the ladder so fast and making so much noise."

"What?"

"Do you want to scare George?"

"I'd never scare George."

"Well, you could have," I said, scanning the floor around the store. "Where is he?"

A faint yip came from inside Aunt Maude's apartment, and I rushed toward the sound. Jim followed along behind me as if he were some sort of self-appointed chaperone.

"I don't need your help, you know."

"Nope, don't suppose you do," he said.

My objections didn't stop him from following me into the apartment. I tried very hard to ignore his unwanted company by not looking back at him.

I found George on the braided rug beside Aunt Maude's bed. He was lying on his stomach with his back legs stretched out behind him, and he greeted me with a wide yawn.

"There you are," I said.

"See, he's okay."

The little dog was panting, and his tongue hung out the side of his mouth. When I knelt down to pet him, he rolled onto his back, offering up his tummy for a rub. I was happy to oblige.

"See how he holds his tongue?" I said. "Can't you see he needs a drink?"

"He's got water in his bowl," he said. "If he needs a drink, he'll get one."

When Jim knelt down beside me to scratch the little pug's ears, George wagged at both of us. The corners of his mouth turned up, and it looked to me as if he were smiling with sheer delight from all the attention.

"He's just fine," Jim said.

I hated to admit George didn't look as though he were suffering from neglect. Reluctantly, I got up and headed back into the store with Jim close behind.

"Isn't this great?" he said. "I'm the one who gets to spend the whole day with George."

I didn't think he could be any more obnoxious, but he proved me wrong. All I could do at that moment was glare at him with the meanest look I could muster. In return, he laughed at me.

"Taking care of George is no laughing matter," I said.

When I turned to leave, he was standing at the end of the counter with an odd twinkle in his eye. It made me want to scream at him and his arrogance, but I wouldn't give him the satisfaction.

I grabbed an apple from a bowl on the end of the counter and took a bite. It was a long time until our two o'clock lunch with Grandma, and I didn't think Aunt Maude would mind if I took just one little apple.

"And remember," I said. "George goes home with me this afternoon."

Before he could say anything in return, I yanked the door open and stormed out of the store. To add emphasis, I let the door slam shut behind me.

"There. That should show him I mean business."

I stood on the sidewalk just outside the store and pulled Grandma's note from my pocket. I barely noticed the people walking around me while I finished the apple and studied the list.

"I wonder what my friends would say if they could see me now."

I tossed the apple core into a wooden barrel next to Jim's bike and jammed the note back inside my pocket. There was a lot to do, so I spun on my heel and headed to the east side of town.

Nineteen

Mr. Martin leaned back in his chair and rubbed his temple with the side of his iced tea glass. Droplets of condensation rolled down the side of his face and onto the collar of his best Sunday shirt.

"It sure did warm up today," he said to himself.

After taking another long drink of the tea, he put the glass down on the side table next to a pad of paper and the stub of a carpenter's pencil. On the paper were several scribbled items in two separate columns.

"Let's see," he said, tapping the paper with his forefinger. "I gotta do everything on this side of the paper fer Mrs. Ivey."

He scratched his head and studied the items in that column. They were things he always did for her. He got the milk, hauled the café's garbage out to the alley and burned it in the trash barrel, kept the front walk swept and ran errands whenever she needed something. Nothing new.

In the other column were the things he needed to do to get ready for the Fourth of July potluck. He knew he would get everything in both columns done, but he worried about everyone else. He hoped all of them remembered to finish their part of the plans.

"Seems like gittin' ready fer the potluck is the easy part," he said. "Keepin' our plans a secret from Mrs. Ivey an' that granddaughter of hers is gonna be the hard part."

He sighed, picked up the glass of tea and took another swallow. Holding the meeting at the café so early that morning and cleaning up everything afterward exhausted him. He didn't bother to tell Mrs. Ivey he went home to take a short nap, but he didn't think she would mind.

"I surely did need some shut eye."

Now that he was rested, he was ready to drive into Lafayette to visit Aunt Maude in the hospital. After that, he planned to buy the café's milk from a dairy in Lafayette instead of Monticello. He didn't figure Mrs. Ivey would mind where he bought it as long as he got milk.

"But ya gotta git home before dark," he said to himself. "Yer old eyes aren't any good fer drivin' at night."

Besides, he promised Clyde he'd go to Monticello the next day to check on the fireworks. He needed to get back in time for a good night's sleep to do that.

The grandfather clock across the living room chimed the hour, and he squinted at the time. It read nine o'clock.

"Time ta git goin'."

He pushed himself up out of the overstuffed chair, took his glass to the kitchen and gave it a quick rinse. Last night's dishes were still stacked in the sink, but he didn't have the energy to wash them.

"I'll sure be glad when the Fourth of July is over," he said. "I'm gittin' too old fer all this."

He stretched his arms out to his sides and stood a little straighter. Several of the bones in his back made loud popping sounds. He ignored the noise, grabbed his old hat from the coat rack by the front door and put it on.

"All the other folks gotta do is git the food together an' decorate the gym," he said. "I gotta figure out how ta keep Mrs. Ivey an' Shirley outa the way all day."

He reached for the ring of keys on a hook beside the front door and secured its chain to his belt. Hoping he hadn't forgotten anything, he walked out to the old truck, eased inside and started the engine. With the usual stubbornness of the transmission, he forced the shift lever into first gear and pointed the truck toward Lafayette.

"Yes, sir," he said. "I gotta figure a way ta keep 'em busy."

Twenty

The first errand on the list took me all the way to Mrs. Van Berkel's farm. Grandma wanted me to buy the freshest eggs available, and she specifically wrote down Mrs. Van Berkel's name.

Her farm was over a mile from the café, so getting the eggs was the only errand on the list I could get done before lunch at two o'clock. But the eggs in the cartons I was carrying were the absolute freshest. I gathered them myself right from under the hens.

I had never been inside a chicken coop before, but Mrs. Van Berkel was extremely patient with me. She spent a lot of time demonstrating how to gather the eggs without disturbing the hens. Of course, she was an expert at it, and I was only an amateur. Never before did I see so many feathers fly or hear so much cackling.

"I'm pretty sure those hens will be okay," I said. "I'm just not too sure about Mrs. Van Berkel."

I walked slower than normal with the cartons of fragile cargo. By the time I reached Willowdale, I was surprised to see how deserted Main Street was. The only thing moving was a truck stacked so high with hay bales it looked as though a light breeze could tip the whole thing over.

As it passed by, a man and three small children waved at me from inside the cab. Of course, I couldn't wave back with my arms full. I wasn't about to risk breaking a single egg.

"If only I had my own car and a driver's license, I could rule the world."

Well, maybe not the world. But if I had a car, I wouldn't have to walk to Mrs. Van Berkel's farm. For sure, my arms wouldn't ache, and my face wouldn't be sweaty and caked with dust.

"If my friends could see me now, they would never believe how awful I look."

When I finally reached the café, I rested the top carton nearest me against my cheek and hooked an index finger around the screen door handle. Just that simple movement caused the stack to wobble.

I held my breath, and the wobbling stopped. I decided it would be safer for the eggs if I yelled for help instead.

"Grandma, are you there?"

I twisted sideways, keeping the stack level. I tried to look inside for her, but the cartons blocked my view. All I knew was I was exhausted, and I needed help right away.

"Grandma!"

Just when I thought I couldn't hold onto the cartons another second, I heard the familiar click of Grandma's shoes. The sound grew closer and closer.

"Ye gods and little fishes," she said. "That's quite the load you have there."

"Uh-huh."

She opened the door for me, but I didn't stop to talk. I stepped around her and walked straight to the kitchen. It would have taken too long to explain about my chicken coop adventure, and my arms cried for relief.

While I held the cartons, Grandma untied the twine holding them together, took one carton at a time and stored each one inside the walk-in cooler. I didn't speak or take a deep breath until every carton was safely put away.

"I didn't realize you went through so many eggs in a week, Grandma."

"Oh, those won't last a week."

I cringed. It was too soon to think about visiting that foul smelling coop and all those cackling hens again. I wasn't even sure if Mrs. Van Berkel would ever be ready for another visit from me.

"I think I'll go clean up a little," I said and headed to the small bathroom beside the back door.

While I washed off my filthy shoes and scrubbed my hands and face, the phone at the end of the counter rang. I heard Grandma answer it, but her voice was too muffled for me to make out anything she said.

I put the call out of my mind, dried my hands and face on a hand towel and brushed a couple of feathers off my skirt. I didn't look as neat and clean as I liked, but it was the best I could do.

When I went back into the dining room, Grandma was off the phone and at the front table arranging three place settings.

The water glass beside each plate reflected a kaleidoscope of color off its beveled surface.

"The table looks really nice, Grandma," I said. "I especially like the floral tablecloth."

She didn't smile or say thank you. She just stepped back and eyed her work.

"It will have to do under the circumstances."

"Under what—circumstances?"

Before she could answer, Jim burst through the front door. His hat was in his hands, and his T-shirt was neatly tucked into the waist of his jeans. I had to admit he looked very handsome for someone so obnoxious.

"Am I late?"

"No," Grandma said. "You're exactly on time."

She walked slower than normal to the front of the dining room, closed the main door and engaged the lock. It was too early to close, so I couldn't understand why she locked the door.

"Is everything okay, Grandma?"

She shrugged her shoulders and let out a long, low sigh. It wasn't like Grandma to be so quiet or so unenthusiastic. I couldn't imagine what was wrong.

"Both of you sit down, please."

Jim and I did as she asked and waited while she paced back and forth between the table and the front door. A few strands of her hair hung from the bun at her neck, but she didn't attempt to tuck them back into place.

Finally, she stopped pacing and pulled out the chair next to Grandpa's. When she sat down, she collapsed onto the chair like a rag doll.

"I'm afraid I have disturbing news about Aunt Maude."

For a few seconds, I sat there unable to comprehend what she said. It was Jim who finally spoke.

"What about Aunt Maude?"

"I received a call from the hospital while Shirley was getting cleaned up."

"Shirley had to get cleaned up?"

"Never mind him, Grandma," I said. "I heard the phone ring a little while ago."

"Dr. Thompson wanted me to know Aunt Maude is more ill than he originally thought."

What? I didn't understand. Until last night, Aunt Maude seemed fine. She even baked cookies and fixed supper for Grandma and me. Besides, Grandma said Aunt Maude was a bit of a hypochondriac.

"The doctor says her heart is very weak, and she won't be able to work again."

Jim and I sat quietly. I didn't know what to say. I didn't know what to think.

"You mean she can't work in the general store anymore?" Jim said.

Grandma sat up a little straighter and tucked one strand of loose hair back into the bun. She smoothed the skirt of her work dress over her knees and looked at me. Then, she looked at Jim.

"I mean, she won't be coming back to Willowdale at all."

Jim let out a gasp, and I looked over at him. His face was as white as one of Grandma's bleached dishtowels.

"But what will happen to her store?" he said.

"I'm afraid she'll have to sell it."

The room grew quiet except for the ticking of the clock on the wall. Time seemed to stand still, yet everything around me changed.

The smell of the chili simmering on the stove in the kitchen should have made my mouth water. After all, Aunt Maude's apple was the only thing I had to eat all day. But the thought of never seeing Aunt Maude again took my appetite away.

"Where will she go?" I said.

"As far as I know, she will be going to live with her brother."

"Where's that?" Jim said.

"In Illinois."

He stood up and turned toward the front window. Since there was no traffic on the street to see, I was sure he just needed a little time to think. His shoulders drooped a little, and his head moved back and forth.

"What's going to happen to George?"

"I don't know, Jimmy," Grandma said. "I don't know any other details."

At least I finally understood why Grandma locked the door and why Main Street was so empty. The whole town probably knew about Aunt Maude. Who could blame them for not

wanting to eat out or go shopping? They were losing a neigh-
bor and a good friend.

Twenty-one

"What a shame about Aunt Maude," he said to himself. "She surely did look sick."

Mr. Martin pulled the old truck into traffic and glanced over at the two crates on the seat next to him. The bottles inside of them were filled with milk for the café.

"That worked out good," he said. "Those folks over ta the dairy were real nice."

He left the hospital before visiting hours ended in order to get to the dairy before closing time. Even so, it was late, and the sun was nearly to the horizon.

"Sure glad I went ta see ya, Aunt Maude," he said, clicking on the headlights. "No tellin' when we'll see ya once yer gone ta yer brother's place."

The traffic on the narrow road was heavy with commuters going home from work, and a line of cars was stacked up behind the old truck. They bobbed in and out of line, trying to pass, but Mr. Martin held his speed at the usual 45 miles an hour.

"Go ahead an' honk," he said. "I'm not gonna speed up fer anybody."

After several minutes of bobbing and weaving, the line of traffic finally got around. As they passed him, Mr. Martin waved and smiled at each one.

"There's no sense in gittin' mad at an old man like me," he said. "Yer gonna be old someday, too."

As the taillights of the passing cars faded away, he squinted at the road ahead. With the sun so low in the sky, the white line in the center of the road was barely visible to him. He eased the truck to the right and followed the brighter line on the side of the road.

"These darn old eyes."

He stepped on the button on the floor, and the bright beams came to life. He ignored the on and off warning blink of headlights from oncoming traffic and followed the white line toward Willowdale.

"It surely was a long day."

His visit with Aunt Maude and buying the milk in Lafayette was all he could handle. He wanted to unload the milk at the café, get home and get to bed. Only the day wasn't quite done thanks to Aunt Maude.

When the traffic thinned out a little, he loosened his tight grip on the wheel and moved his right hand to the pocket of his dress shirt. He patted the pieces of paper inside and shook his head.

Aunt Maude had written three notes. Each one of them was addressed to a different friend in Willowdale. Because she was going straight to her brother's when she was released from the hospital, she asked him to deliver them for her.

"Glad ta do it," he said. "But ya sure got me curious about what ya wrote."

He put his hand back on the wheel and concentrated on his driving. By maintaining his usual low speed, it took him almost an hour to reach the outskirts of Willowdale. By then, the streetlights were on, and the light on top of the water tower was blinking on and off.

"That surely is a welcome sight."

He loved seeing all the lights, but he still had the notes to deliver. He turned left at the next gravel road and headed toward the old mill.

"I'll git Jimmy's ta him first," he said. "I'll git Mrs. Ivey's ta her after I git this milk ta the café."

With the bright beams still on, he aimed the truck down the center of the dusty road and maintained an even distance between the side ditches. There was no moonlight to help guide him, so he bumped along at 10 miles an hour, steadying the crates with one hand.

"I'm not openin' my note 'til I git home," he said. "It's a real treat gittin' a note from a friend."

Tomorrow, he would plan his trip into Monticello to buy the supplies and check on the fireworks. Right then, he was too tired to think about shopping.

Twenty-two

Irene cooked so much chili for our lunch with Jim there was more than enough for both lunch and supper. But none of us was hungry after we heard the news about Aunt Maude.

In order not to waste food, Grandma divided the chili into two containers. One was for Jim and his father. The other was for Grandma and me.

Since neither of us ate breakfast that morning, I knew Grandma and I needed to eat something soon. When Jim went back to the general store and Grandma started work on the ledger, I went home to put the chili on the stove to simmer.

I set the dining room table with Grandma's good dishes and arranged the linen napkins she liked to use beside each place setting. Hoping to lift her spirits a little, I arranged a few roses from the flower garden in her favorite vase. They looked beautiful in the center of the table.

"Grandma sure is going to be surprised."

I checked my watch. It was time to get back to town and pick up George. I figured Jim wouldn't keep the general store open waiting for me to arrive, and I certainly wasn't going to give him the satisfaction of taking George home with him for the night.

"Get moving," I said to myself. "You can't be late."

I hurried to my bedroom and threw on a pair of blue jeans and an old baggy blouse. As far as I was concerned, there was no need to stay in my work clothes. I didn't know how Grandma would feel about it, but I was sure George wouldn't mind.

When I got back downstairs, I took one last look at the table and checked the pot on the stove. Everything looked ready.

With nothing left to do, I ran out the back door and down the driveway. At the county road, I only stopped long enough to catch my breath. Then, I ran along the side of the gravel road toward Willowdale.

"I wish my friends could see me now," I said, "They'd never believe I'm actually running somewhere."

I didn't waste more time by taking another break along the way, and I was sorry I didn't. By the time I reached the café, my sides hurt, my lungs burned and my throat was on fire.

"Way—to—go,—Shirley."

I leaned my hand against the far corner of the café where Grandma couldn't see me, and I gasped for air. Right then and there, I decided I wasn't track team material.

When I was able to take a full breath again, I looked up at the water tower. The light on top was blinking even though it wasn't dark enough, and it looked just as sad as always with the faded lettering.

"Why doesn't somebody put a new coat of paint on the poor thing?" I said. "How hard could it be?"

Up and down Main Street, the stores were closed for the day except for the café and the general store, and the streetlights were on. That didn't make sense. It wasn't dark enough for them to be on, too.

The only thing moving was a truck turning onto a gravel road west of town. It had its bright headlights on.

"Shirley," Grandma said from inside the café. "Is that you?"

"Yes, Grandma, I'm coming."

I took a deep breath and went inside, but when I saw Grandma, I stopped short. She stood beside the front table with her arms folded across her chest. Her toe was tapping against the floor.

"Jimmy is waiting to close up," she said. "Are you finally ready?"

What did she mean by finally? I wanted to tell her I had already been home, put supper on the stove and was back in record time. But I didn't want to spoil the surprise. What I did want to do was sit down and rest for a minute.

Instead, Grandma steered me back outside and locked the door behind us. On the other side of the street, Jim stood outside the general store with George in tow with one hand and the container of chili in the other.

As we crossed the street toward them, the little pug pulled on the leash and wagged at Grandma and me. He wagged so hard, Jim struggled to keep from dropping the container.

"Easy there, George," he said. "I only have two hands."

"Hi, big guy," I said. "You ready to go home?"

While I patted George on the head and took the leash from Jim, Grandpa's old truck rounded the corner at the end of Main Street. Its bright headlights were on.

Mr. Martin honked at us and brought the truck to a stop parallel to the curb. The three of us stepped to the edge of the sidewalk and leaned over to look through the open passenger window. George sat down at my feet.

"I tried ta git ya at home, Jimmy, but yer dad said I'd find ya here."

"Yeah," he said. "I had to wait for Shirley."

I stood up straight and glared at him. Did everyone think I just sat around all day and did nothing?

"Glad yer still here," he said. "I got somethin' fer both of ya from Aunt Maude."

Grandma's face lit up with a wide smile. She looked hopeful.

"How is she, Mr. Martin?"

"Not so good," he said. "She's still goin' ta Illinois ta live with her brother."

Grandma's smile disappeared. She stood up and let out a small groan, but Jim stayed at the window.

"What do you have for us?"

From inside his shirt pocket, Mr. Martin pulled out two folded pieces of paper. He reached across the two crates of milk and handed them to Jim. He kept one and handed the other one to Grandma.

"She said there's somethin' she needed ta ask ya."

Grandma turned her note around in her hands, and Jim just stared at his. Since neither of them said a word, I felt obligated to say something.

"Thank you, Mr. Martin."

That didn't seem quite adequate after he went to so much trouble going to Lafayette and back. But it was all I could think to say.

"Well, then," he said. "I'm gonna put the milk away."

When he didn't get any response from Grandma or Jim, he forced the shift lever into first gear, did a U-turn in the middle of the street and drove around the corner to the alley behind the café. Grandma and Jim were so preoccupied with their notes I didn't think they even noticed.

"Aren't you going to read it, Grandma?"

She finally stopped inspecting the note and looked up at me. Her eyes were brimming with tears.

"It's time we go home, dear."

Jim sniffed a little and wiped his nose on the back of his hand. He stuffed Aunt Maude's note into a back pocket of his jeans.

"Yeah," he said. "I have to get home and heat up the chili for Dad and me."

Without another word, he grabbed his bike with his free hand, eased onto the seat and slowly pedaled up the street. George tugged on his leash trying to follow him, but I held him back. It seemed Jim didn't have the manners to say goodbye to any of us.

"That was sure rude," I said.

143

Grandma touched my arm, and I looked over at her. Her tears were gone, and the self-assured grandmother I knew and loved was back.

"Don't be so hard on the boy," she said. "He thinks of Aunt Maude as his second mother."

With that, she spun around and headed toward home. She walked so fast, George and I struggled to keep up.

By the time we reached the end of the sidewalk, George was panting so hard I worried he might pass out. Grandma didn't seem to notice, so I picked him up, gave him a huge hug and carried him the rest of the way home.

Twenty-three

I waited for over a week, but Grandma never told me what Aunt Maude wrote in her note. Even Jim was silent about his, but I never expected him to discuss anything with me.

"Well, George," I said. "I wonder if you and I will ever know what those notes said."

I glanced at the little pug under the kitchen table and listened to his rhythmic snoring. Nothing seemed to disturb him on that gorgeous Sunday morning. Not even the sounds coming from Grandma's bedroom.

For several minutes, I heard drawers open and close and shoes scrape back and forth across floor. Above all that noise, she hummed a monotonous, nonsensical tune.

"I can't imagine what she's doing in there, big guy."

George let out a small whimper, and I bent over the edge of the table to watch him. His wrinkled forehead twitched up and down, and he kicked his little feet in midair as if he were running after something.

"You must be having a wonderful dream."

Ever since Aunt Maude left the hospital and went to live with her brother in Illinois, I worried about George. Jim still watched him during the day, and Grandma and I still took him home every afternoon. But what was going to happen to him when summer was over? Who was going to take care of him then?

"What do you think, George?"

The noise in the bedroom stopped, and the door opened a crack. Grandma, dressed in her bathrobe and slippers, stood close to the opening. She purposely blocked my view of her room.

"Breakfast is ready, Grandma."

"I'm not very hungry this morning," she said. "You go ahead and finish eating without me."

She ducked back inside her bedroom and clicked the door shut behind her. The same shoe scraping and humming began again.

It wasn't like Grandma to skip her morning cup of coffee, and I couldn't begin to guess what she was up to. So, I finished my cereal and carried my dirty bowl to the sink. In case Grandma changed her mind, I left her bowl and coffee cup on the table.

"I'm going to get dressed now, George."

I checked to see if he heard me, but my voice must not have registered. His feet still churned the air, and his eyelids fluttered.

"I'll be right back," I said, just in case.

With Grandma still humming away inside her room, I wandered upstairs and opened the bottom drawer of my desk. My savings account book was on top of the manila envelope full of my daily letters.

I picked up the little book and turned to the first page. There, written in black ink, was a list of all the money I earned so far. Plus a little bit of interest the bank paid me.

"Just look at that," I said, running my finger across the entries. "At 45 cents an hour, I'll have more than enough money by the end of summer to get my class sweater and ring."

Grandma had insisted I open the account when I first arrived in Willowdale, and I was glad she did. I didn't want to spend any of my earnings before I got home.

"My friends will be jealous when they find out I have my own money."

I dropped the book on top of the manila envelope and closed the drawer. At the same time, the scent of lilacs drifted through the open window, and I took a deep breath of the sweet smell.

"It's too nice to be inside on such a pretty day."

I hurried over to the tiny closet across the room and rummaged through my clothes. I found my favorite pair of shorts and matching shirt and changed out of my pajamas.

When I was finished dressing and pulling my hair into a pony tail, I slipped into my moccasins and ran back downstairs. I looked under the table to check on George, but he wasn't there. I found him curled up on his blanket inside the cardboard pen.

"Oh, no, George," I said. "It's way too nice to stay here."

I carried him outside and placed him next to me on the tree swing. Tucking my left foot underneath me, I pumped the swing into motion with my right foot.

"What do you think we should do today?"

I smiled down at the little dog, but he was asleep. Neither my voice nor the warm breeze ruffling the thick mane around his neck seemed to bother him.

"If I was—were at home right now, Mom and I would probably take a drive in the country."

George flailed his legs, pushed his feet against the backrest and rolled onto his back. I reached over and stopped him from rolling off the edge of the moving swing.

"I bet you'd like a ride in the county, wouldn't you?"

He answered with a loud snort followed by a soft snore. His broad chest, a lighter shade of brown from the rest of his hair, slowly rose and fell with each breath.

"Don't worry," I said. "I know we don't have a car, but I'll think of something else to do."

I pumped the swing with my foot and listened to the birds chirping in the branches above us. It was so peaceful, I could almost visualize Grandpa sitting beside me and counting cars on the county road. The way we used to when I was a little girl.

On the verge of dozing off, I gazed through half-closed eyes out across the yard and the cornfield to the county road beyond. There were very few cars for me to count.

Just as my eyes were about to close completely, I noticed a cloud of dust billowing up along a side road. Grandpa's old truck, running ahead of the cloud, turned onto the county road without stopping at the intersection.

At first, it seemed the truck was headed toward town. Instead, it turned at Grandma's driveway and started up the hill toward her house. My eyes popped wide open, and I sat up straight.

"What do you suppose Mr. Martin's doing here on Sunday?"

George snorted, opened his eyes and flipped onto his stomach. I reached for him, pulled him onto my lap and watched the truck bounce up the driveway.

"Shirley?"

I wrapped my arms around George and eased off the swing. Grandma was standing on the porch, watching us.

She was wearing a bright yellow sundress and a straw hat with a wide brim. A wicker basket was in one hand and a beach towel was in the other. Unlike a workday, her hair hung over her shoulder in a single braid.

"What is it, Grandma?"

"Mr. Martin is coming to take us to Lake Sullivan for a picnic," she said. "Come and put on your bathing suit."

"Really?"

"Hurry, now," she said. "I've already prepared our lunch."

I ran up the porch steps and put George down at her feet. I threw my arms around her neck and gave her a quick hug.

"You're the best."

"Ye gods," she said. "Go get changed."

I ran upstairs and put on my one-piece swimsuit and a pink terry cloth cover-up. I exchanged my moccasins for a pair of sandals.

By the time I got back downstairs, Grandma and Mr. Martin were already inside the cab of the truck. George was squeezed between them, staring out the windshield with wide eyes.

"Good morning, Mr. Martin."

"Jump in the back," he said. "We got one stop ta make."

I climbed into the bed of the truck and sandwiched myself between two folded canvas chairs and Grandma's wicker basket. I didn't know what the one stop was, but I loved picnics. And I loved surprises.

Imagine my surprise when we drove to the mill and stopped in front of Jim's house. He was outside the yard gate wearing a striped T-shirt and green swim trunks. There was an ice chest on the ground next to his bare feet.

"Mornin', Jimmy," Mr. Martin said.

"Hey, Mr. Martin. Mrs. Ivey."

"There's plenty of room in the back," Grandma said. "Make yourself comfortable."

I couldn't believe my bad luck. All I wanted was one day of the week when I didn't have to put up with Jim, but I knew I didn't have a choice.

I scooted closer to the cab and pulled the folding chairs along with me. Jim wrestled the cooler over the tailgate and dropped it into the extra space. He leaped in beside it, shoved the wicker basket out of his way and settled down on the opposite side of the truck from me.

"Is your dad coming?" I said.

"Nope, he's at an auction today."

150

"That's too bad."

Mr. Martin leaned his head out the window and looked back at us. He wasn't wearing his old felt hat. In its place, he wore a light brown canvas hat. Around the band dangled an assortment of fishhooks and lures.

"Hang on back there," he said. "This could git a little bumpy."

Twenty-four

Mr. Martin was right about the Lake Sullivan road. It was extremely bumpy, and so was everything else about the ride.

Jim and I didn't speak to each other the whole time. We sat on our opposite sides of the truck, staring out at the passing scenery and avoiding eye contact.

When we finally got to the lake, Mr. Martin drove the truck onto the beach and parked in the shade of a sprawling willow tree. Several trucks and cars were parked among the other trees, and a group of small children ran up and down the sand, screaming and playing with a beach ball.

The tension between Jim and me threatened to spoil a perfectly beautiful day, but I wasn't about to let that happen. I jumped out of the truck before the engine ping stopped and ran up to the driver's window.

"This oughta be a good spot ta park," Mr. Martin said.

"I agree."

"I do, too, Grandma."

As Jim and Mr. Martin unloaded the truck, Grandma and I unfolded the two canvas chairs and spread a blanket on the sand. George waited near the tree's broad trunk while we worked. When everything was in place, he slogged over to the blanket and plopped down next to the wicker basket on the edge of the blanket.

"Well, now," Mr. Martin said. "That's all the work I'm fixin' ta do."

He eased onto one of the chairs, leaned back and tilted his fishing hat against the sun's glare off the water. Within seconds, he was snoring.

Instead of sitting on the other canvas chair, Grandma knelt down and slid onto the blanket. When she was settled, George rolled over and snuggled up next to her.

The prospect of sitting next to George was very tempting, but I wasn't ready to sit down. There was too much activity on the beach to sit and just watch. I wanted to be a part of it.

"This was a wonderful idea, Grandma."

"Actually, it was Mr. Martin who suggested it."

It was hard to believe Mr. Martin wanted to take time from his one day of rest to drive all of us to the lake. Of course, I imagined he might want to spend time with Grandma and Jim, but I knew I was only a nuisance to him. Someone he tolerated out of respect for Grandma.

Jim stood a few feet away from me with his hands on his hips. He moved his head back and forth, scanning the lake and the beach area.

"Enough of this standing around," he said. "Who's ready for a swim?"

Without waiting for an answer, he slipped out of his T-shirt and started toward the water. Halfway there, he caught a ball some older boys were keeping away from a young girl and handed it to her.

"Thanks, mister," she said.

"Hey, that's not fair," one of the boys said.

"Tough."

I didn't know whether he was helping the girl or being obnoxious to the boy. Either way, he strutted past the group and never looked back.

"Shirley, go ahead and take a swim," Grandma said. "Have some fun."

"I think I will."

"Just don't swim too long. You should have something to eat soon."

I kicked off my sandals, tossed my cover-up on the blanket and ran to the water's edge. Jim was waiting for me, but I ignored him.

I wound my way past a group of wading children and pushed through the water until I was waist deep. A few seconds later, Jim plunged in right beside me, spraying water everywhere.

"Last one back to the beach is a monkey's uncle," he said.

"What's that supposed to mean?"

"It means I bet I can swim to the dive platform and back before you can."

"You're on."

Before I could even take my first stroke, he dived under the water. When he surfaced several feet ahead of me, his arms were already pumping and propelling him through the choppy water. His crawl stroke was strong, and his form was perfect.

"You didn't say to go!"

I dived right in and chased after him. I learned to swim when I was practically a baby, so I was pretty good at it. But as fast as I swam, he swam faster. Thanks to his superior speed and unfair start, I struggled to catch up to him.

Just when I thought there was no hope for me, I remembered what I learned at camp. I coordinated my arms with my breathing and double stroked between breaths. Although that kept the drag of the water at a minimum, Jim pulled even farther ahead.

After fighting through his wake and swallowing some lake water in the process, I got to the floating platform a few seconds after he did. He was wearing his obnoxious smile and hanging onto a cleat by one hand.

"Thought you'd never get here," he said.

Instead of stopping, I kicked my legs harder to maintain my momentum. I tapped the side of the platform, did a racing turn and swam back toward shore at full speed.

"Hey, wait a sec.," he said. "That's cheating."

Even though I swam as fast as I could, Jim passed me, and his wake hit me in the face. This time, I held my breath to keep the water out of my mouth, and I kicked even harder.

About halfway back to shore, a young boy fell off his inner tube. The rubber donut shot into Jim's path, forcing him to veer off course. I took full advantage of the distraction.

I increased the speed of my strokes, kicked as hard as I could and pulled ahead of him. When I reached shallow water first, I stood up and shouted so everyone could hear.

"I win! I win!"

I shoved my way through the last few feet to the shore, creating a wake. Behind me, I heard Jim moaning.

"That's not fair," he said. "I demand a rematch."

"Tough."

I ignored him and his petty complaint and struggled through the deep sand on the beach. When I reached our blanket, I dropped to my hands and knees in front of Grandma. I struggled to get a full breath.

"Who—do you—say won, Grandma?"

Her face was hidden from me behind the brim of her straw hat. With a half-eaten sandwich in her hand, she laughed so hard she couldn't speak. George, still curled up in the center of the blanket, opened his eyes and wagged at me.

"Mr. Martin?" I said.

"No doubt about it," he said, nodding his head. "It was Jimmy."

"What?"

I took a towel from a stack of them beside Grandma, sat on the edge of the blanket and dried the water off of my arms and legs. Jim flopped down on the sand in front of me, grinning.

"Well, I'd like a second opinion," I said.

I looked at Grandma again. Her laughing slowed to a giggle, and she adjusted her hat's brim so I could see her face.

"Well, Grandma?"

"I'd have to say it was a tie."

"That does it," I said. "I demand a rematch, too."

"Not until I get something to eat," Jim said. "A guy could starve."

He reached for the wicker basket, threw open the wooden lid and shuffled through the contents. After retrieving two sandwiches and an apple, he slammed the lid closed. He held the food close to his chest, crawled on his knees to the empty canvas chair and rolled onto its sling seat.

I ignored his rudeness and helped myself to one of the remaining sandwiches and a pop from the ice chest. George rolled onto his back, making room for me on the blanket.

"Hi, big guy."

I set the bottle of pop on the blanket and pulled the waxed paper off my sandwich. Just as I suspected, it was filled with peanut butter and jelly.

"You must have spent hours preparing our gourmet lunch, Grandma."

"You're just fortunate I didn't have time to prepare potato salad, young lady."

Tilting his hat up a little, Mr. Martin grinned and said, "Thank yer lucky stars."

All of us laughed at him, and about a minute later, he was asleep again with his hat pulled over his face. In order not to disturb him, Grandma and Jim and I watched the children play on the beach while we ate our sandwiches.

When Grandma finished eating, she kicked off her sandals and lay down on the blanket next to George. She tilted her hat over her face, and within seconds, she was snoring softly.

I wrapped my towel around my shoulders and scanned the beach. Some of the parents hid under brightly colored umbrellas while their children built sand castles. Others held smaller children in their arms and jumped incoming waves.

Jim was leaned back in the chair with his eyes closed and his arms folded across his bare chest. The dappled shade of the willow tree protected him from the bright sun.

"Are you asleep?" I said to him.

"Not really."

"Would you like another sandwich?"

"No."

"Do you want a towel?"

"No."

I struggled for something else to say. Finally, I latched onto a subject I was certain he would enjoy. Himself.

"Aunt Maude says you're planning to go to college."

"Yeah," he said. "Purdue."

"Not me," I said. "I'm going to Ball State."

He opened his eyes and rolled his head to one side. He looked straight at me.

"You're going to be a teacher?"

"I guess so," I said. "That's what Mom thinks I should be."

"Your mom thinks?"

"She says it's a good job for a woman."

"I suppose."

159

"Why are you going to Purdue?"

"I'm going to be an engineer."

"An engineer?" I said. "Wow."

I was truly impressed. None of my friends thought past the next football game or Friday night dance. In fact, my girl-friends were more concerned about the latest fashions than future careers.

"I think I can get a scholarship and maybe get a job on campus," he said.

"Wow."

"With that and my savings, I should be able to swing it."

I saw an earnest look on his face. He had never spoken so seriously before, and I could tell the subject had deep meaning for him.

"Is that why you're working for your grandmother this summer?" he said.

"What?"

"Are you working for her to earn money for college?"

I looked away from him and toward the lake. I didn't think he'd like the real answer. So, I lied.

"Sure."

He didn't seem to hear me. Instead, he changed the subject completely.

"Now, if I could just figure out what to do about George," he said.

"What do you mean?"

"Aunt Maude wants me to keep him after you leave."

My mouth dropped open. I was hurt she didn't ask me to take him home, but I didn't say anything. I waited for him to continue.

"Her note said she thinks I'd give him a good home."

If that's what was in the note, he should have sounded happier. I couldn't imagine why he didn't.

"You're really lucky she wants you to have him."

"Yeah, I am," he said. "Except that we can't afford to keep him."

My mouth dropped open again. I began to feel like a hungry Venus's-flytrap the way my mouth dropped open so often.

Although I didn't like it, I had to agree Jim was the best choice to take the little pug if I couldn't. But what would happen to George if he couldn't afford to keep him?

"There must be something you can do," I said.

Before Jim had time to answer, George woke up with a yawn. He groaned a little and rolled onto his stomach. His tongue hung from his mouth, and he panted heavily.

"Grandma," I said. "George is getting too hot."

She tipped her hat away from her face and sat up. Her braid hung in front of her, and she flipped it back over her shoulder.

"Well, everyone," she said. "Time to go home."

While she struggled to stand up, I draped my damp towel across George's back and carried him to the truck. The front seat was in the shade and a soft breeze blew through the open door. I offered him some water, but he refused to drink. He sprawled across the seat with the wind blowing in his face and panted.

"We'll be home soon, big guy," I said. "I promise."

With all of us helping, it only took a few minutes to reload the truck with all of our belongings. As Mr. Martin drove us back to Willowdale, I kept a close eye on George through the rear window of the cab.

Twenty-five

Grandma left early for the café, so George and I had the whole house to ourselves before I had to be at work. It was a nice, quiet way to start the day, but I couldn't imagine why Grandma left without me. All she said was she had to attend to some business or other.

"Well, George," I said. "It must be pretty important for her to miss breakfast again."

The little pug snorted at me and spun in a slow, tight circle. It was his usual happy dance before every meal, and he kept an eye on the bag of dog food on the table.

"Are you hungry?"

Of course, he was hungry. Grandma always said breakfast was the most important meal of the day. For George, every meal was the most important.

"Okay, okay. I'm almost done."

I finished washing and rinsing my juice glass and cereal bowl and wiped my hands on the dishtowel. George yipped at me.

"Now it's your turn."

I opened the bag of dog food and scooped his morning ration into his bowl. As soon as I set it on the floor, he buried his face in the kibble and ate so fast it looked as though he inhaled the food instead of chewing it.

"What's your hurry?" I said. "You know I'm not going to take it away from you."

He ignored me and finished in record time. After licking every crumb from the bottom of the bowl, he looked up at me and burped.

"Oh, George."

I rinsed his food bowl in hot water. Then, I ran the water until it was cold enough to refill his other bowl. When I finally turned off the faucet, I heard the constant beep of a car horn in the direction of the county road.

"What in the world?"

I looked out the kitchen window and saw Grandpa's truck winding its way up the driveway. The horn never stopped honking.

"What do you suppose that's all about?"

The old truck pulled to a stop a few feet from the back porch with a cloud of dust settling around it. Before the engine stopped pinging, the driver's door flew open, and Jim jumped out.

"Hey, Shirley," he said. "I got my driver's license."

I opened the screen door, and George and I walked outside. The little dog stood at my side, staring at Jim and cocking his head back and forth.

"Really?"

"Yeah," he said, waving a piece of paper in the air. "Your grandma let us borrow the truck yesterday."

"She did?"

"Yeah," he said. "Mr. Martin and I drove to Monticello, and I got perfect scores on everything."

That figured. First, he swam better than I did. Then, he got his driver's license before I did and with perfect scores. Was I ever going to do something better than Jim? The real question was, When did I begin to care if I did?

Mr. Martin leaned out the passenger window and tipped his hat in my direction. Even he was grinning.

"We came ta give ya a ride ta town."

I stepped off the porch and walked over to Jim at the open driver's door. George followed at my heel and wagged enthusiastically.

I was so jealous of Jim at that moment I had an urge to scream. The last thing I wanted to do was give him the satisfaction of taking me for a ride.

"That's alright," I said. "George and I don't mind walking."

"Ah, come on, Shirley," Jim said. "Don't be a spoilsport."

Mr. Martin stepped out of the truck. Without saying a word, he held the passenger door open and motioned for me to get in.

"But I'm not ready for work."

"You look fine to me," Jim said.

I knew my excuses for not going sounded feeble. I picked up George, walked around to the passenger door and slid across to the center of the seat.

"I guess it wouldn't hurt just this once."

With my legs squeezed to the right side of the gear shift lever, I perched George on my lap. Mr. Martin climbed in beside me, and Jim took his place behind the wheel. Both doors slammed shut.

"Are you ready?" Jim said.

I leaned against the seat back and sighed. George sat up straight and looked over his shoulder at me. His tongue hung out, and the corners of his mouth turned up as if he were smiling.

"I guess we're ready," I said.

Jim started the engine. By forcing the shift lever in and out of every gear to jockey the truck forward and backward, he managed to get us turned around. I studied his technique while he drove us down the driveway. I hated to admit he was a pretty good driver.

When we got onto the county road and got closer to town, some of the drivers in the oncoming traffic honked at us when they saw Jim behind the wheel. Each time, Jim waved out the window at them.

We were almost to the café before Mr. Martin said anything. When he did, he sounded serious.

"It surely is a shame."

"A shame?" Jim said.

"It's a shame ya have ta ride that old bike of yers."

"What do you mean?"

Mr. Martin leaned forward and looked around George and me. He adjusted his hat and cleared his throat.

"After we drop Shirley off, let's load up yer papers in the back of this truck."

"What?" I said.

"Jimmy's runnin' kinda late today," he said. "I'm thinkin' yer grandma won't mind me helpin' him a little with his route."

"What?"

I felt my face turn red. Grandma didn't give him Grandpa's truck to do Jim's work, but it wasn't my place to allow what they wanted to do or not. I kept my mouth shut, squirmed a little and nearly knocked George on the floor.

"Hang on, big guy," I said. "We're having another bumpy ride."

Mr. Martin leaned back against the seat again, slipped his hat off his head and brushed at some dust trapped in the creases of the felt. We rode in silence for several minutes before he spoke again.

"Yes, sir, it's been a lota years since I run a paper route around these parts."

"You used to have a route?" Jim said.

"Could be kinda fun ta do it agin."

That did it. I was furious at them for conspiring to take advantage of Grandma's generosity. At that very moment, I vowed to get my license right after my birthday and do the driving for Grandma myself.

"Shirley," Jim said. "You mind taking George to the store for me?"

167

I gave the pug a long hug, and he licked my ear. I was mad at them not George, and I would do anything for Aunt Maude's little dog. What else could I say?

"No, I don't mind."

"Thanks," he said. "Your grandma has a key to the front door."

Twenty-six

Marie sat at the end of the lunch counter on one of the padded stools. The telephone receiver was braced between her chin and shoulder, and she sipped a cup of coffee. She waited while Harriet connected her call to the president of the Monticello chapter of the Central Indiana Men's Association.

"Well, Harriet," she said. "He should be answering his phone by now."

"It's ringing, Marie," the operator said. "But it is a little early to be making a call."

"Ye gods and little fishes, Harriet," she said. "It's almost seven o'clock."

"Exactly."

"If I'm at work by this hour, a pharmacist should be, too."

After several more rings, Mr. McNary picked up the phone on his end of the line. Marie put her coffee cup on the counter and placed the receiver tighter to her ear.

"Hello?"

"Bob, it's Marie."

"Marie Ivey?"

"Of course," she said. "I'm calling about the fireworks."

"You want to talk about fireworks at this hour in the morning?"

"I don't have a lot of time before Shirley gets here, so I have to talk quickly."

"You're at the café?"

"Where else would I be?"

There was a long pause. She took another sip of coffee and waited.

"What is it I can do for you, Marie?"

"It's vital we resume our original plans for the Fourth of July fireworks."

There was another pause. Mr. McNary cleared his throat, and his voice was louder and stronger when he spoke again.

"Didn't you call just yesterday to tell me you didn't want to have the fireworks in Willowdale?"

"I didn't want them here while Maude was in the hospital and so ill."

"Does this mean she's feeling better?"

"Unfortunately, she isn't."

There was another pause. Again, Mr. McNary cleared his throat.

"I'm confused," he said. "If she's still so sick, what's changed your mind about the fireworks?"

"Maude wrote me a note."

"Go on."

"She asked me not to change the plans for the fireworks."

"Oh?"

"She didn't want to be the reason the fun was spoiled for everyone or the surprise was spoiled for Shirley. So, I've reconsidered."

170

There was another pause. The sound of rustling papers crackled through the phone's receiver, and Marie winced at the noise.

"Well, look at that," he said. "The invoice says the fireworks are still being delivered to Willowdale High School."

"That's wonderful!"

"Just one thing," he said. "You'll need someone at the school the afternoon of the fourth when the pyrotechnic experts arrive."

"I assure you, Bob, I've already arranged for someone to be there."

Marie eased off the stool and paced back and forth along the length of the counter. The clicking of her shoes on the wooden floor echoed through the dining room.

"Does this mean our members and their families are still invited?" he said.

Marie stopped pacing and lifted the cup of coffee to her lips. She grimaced and put the cup on the counter without taking a drink.

"Of course, Bob," she said. "Everyone is welcome."

Twenty-seven

With only two days left until the Fourth of July, Mr. Martin called everyone to meet with him one last time. He needed to know if all their plans were set for the potluck and the fireworks.

"Gotta be sure, ya know," he said to himself. "Sometimes folks need a little push."

He pulled into the church parking lot and stopped the old truck in the usual place outside the Sunday school entrance. Before getting out, he scanned the area to make sure he was out of sight of the café.

"I'm gittin' too old fer all this sneakin' around."

When he was satisfied the way was clear, he walked up to the church and knocked on the door. It swung open immediately, and Pastor Lawrence let him inside.

"I hope the same room will be alright," the pastor said.

"Yes, sir, an' thanks fer havin' us agin."

"You know you're welcome here."

Once they reached the meeting room, the pastor sat down on one of the folding chairs, but Mr. Martin wasn't sure if he should sit down, too. Instead, he walked to the window behind the front table and kneaded the battered brim of his hat.

"Ya know," he said. "We woulda had this meetin' at the café, but Mrs. Ivey wanted ta be there real early."

"She did?"

"She's callin' that Bob McNary in Monticello about the fireworks," he said. "She thinks she's gotta git 'em back on track."

"She thinks she does?"

"Yes, sir."

"I don't understand."

"She's got no idea they weren't canceled."

"That's very interesting."

"An' she's got no idea the potluck's all planned."

"No?"

"It's all real complicated."

He walked back to the first row of chairs and sat down. He could see from the pastor's expression he was a little confused.

"Ya see," he said. "Mrs. Ivey wanted to cancel the potluck 'cause of Aunt Maude bein' sick."

"I see."

"But I got the folks around here ta ignore her an' go ahead with the potluck anyways."

"You did?"

"Then, Aunt Maude wrote me a note."

"A note?"

"She wrote notes ta me an' Mrs. Ivey an' Jimmy even before I got ta the hospital."

"Can I ask what your note said?"

"It said about the same thing."

"The same thing?"

"Yes, sir," he said. "She told me ta go ahead with the pot-luck even before she knew I was doin' it anyways."

"Then, making this a surprise for both of them instead of just Shirley was really your idea."

"Yes, sir," he said. "All the folks thought it was a real good one."

"It was, indeed."

"An' Aunt Maude's keepin' it a surprise, too."

"That's why you're meeting here today," the pastor said. "To make sure all the plans are in place."

"That's it to a T, Pastor."

"It seems you have everything well in hand, Mr. Martin."

"That's what I thought."

"Oh?"

"I got a call from Mrs. Ivey last night."

"I don't think I understand."

Mr. Martin stood up and walked to the window again. Since there wasn't any traffic to watch, he turned back to the pastor.

"She told me she changed her mind about not havin'the fireworks, an' she's takin' care 'em."

"She's taking care of them even though they were never canceled in the first place?"

"Yes, sir."

The pastor put his hands on either side of his head and rubbed his temples. He let out a long, low-pitched whistle.

"I can only imagine how confused Mr. McNary must be."

"Yes, sir."

The pastor dropped his hands to his lap and stared up at him. His head nodded slowly up and down.

"And she still doesn't know the potluck is planned?"

"No, sir."

"You're right, Mr. Martin, it is complicated."

"That's not all, Pastor."

"There's more?"

"She wants me ta be at the school when the fireworks folks git there."

"I can't think of a better person for the job."

"But ya see, Pastor, we already got our jobs ta do."

"Of course."

"My job is ta keep Mrs. Ivey an' that granddaughter of hers away from the school."

"Oh?"

"We don't want 'em to see us gittin' ready fer the potluck."

"No, you don't."

"But I sure as shootin' can't be doin' two jobs at the same time."

"That is a dilemma."

Mr. Martin walked across the room again. This time, he put his hat on the empty front table. When he looked up at the window, Jimmy Spencer rode past on his bicycle. One of the saddlebags was full of papers. The other was empty and flapped in the wind.

"Ya know, Pastor," he said. "There's somethin' Shirley wants fer her birthday."

"Oh?"

"Yes, sir," he said. "She wants her driver's license."

"That sounds perfectly normal for a young person."

He left his hat on the table and sat down next to the pastor. He looked the man in the eye.

"Well, we can't git her that."

"No, we certainly can't."

"But maybe we can git her somethin' pretty close," he said. "Maybe solve my own problem, too."

"Oh?"

"I'd need yer help, fer sure."

"What kind of help?"

"Got a driver's license, Pastor?"

"I do, indeed."

"Then, I got just the job fer ya."

Twenty-eight

July fourth was living up to its reputation. The sun was rising in a clear, blue sky, and it was already heating up. Mr. Martin rolled down the driver's window and let the morning air blow in.

"Gonna be a scorcher," he said to himself.

His last meeting at the church went so well it made him feel like a young man again. Everyone there knew his part in the plan, and all the parts were in motion for the biggest surprise potluck and fireworks display ever seen in Willowdale.

He felt so happy about how everything was going, he wanted to sing clear to the heavens, but he couldn't carry a tune. Instead, he hummed a silly jingle he heard once on Aunt Maude's television.

"It was real nice of the pastor ta help me out with Mrs. Ivey an' Shirley."

Since he no longer needed to be in two places at once, he didn't drive down Main Street or stop at the café. He drove straight to the high school from his house. The back of the truck was full of the decorating materials he bought in Monticello.

The parking lot was empty when he got there, but he knew it wouldn't be for very long. The pyrotechnic people were scheduled to arrive in a short while, and the townsfolk planned to decorate the gym after that. Thanks to the pastor's help, the only job left for him to do was to unlock the gym and greet the fireworks experts.

"If the pastor does his job right," he said, "Mrs. Ivey an' that granddaughter of hers won't see a thing that's goin' on over here."

Instead of choosing a parking spot, he circled the perimeter of the dusty lot. He drove to the side of the high school building and stopped the truck at the side entrance to the gym.

"This oughta be good," he said. "Easy ta unload from here."

He got out of the truck, walked up to the gym door and fumbled with his ring of keys. When he found the one he needed, he opened the lock, but he didn't have a chance to go inside. A moving van with "Indiana Pyrotechnics, Inc." written on its side pulled into the lot.

The driver stopped only a few feet from Mr. Martin and leaned his head out the window. When he spoke, he practically yelled.

"Is this where the fireworks are supposed to go?"

He laughed, went over to the van and shook the driver's hand. The other two men inside only nodded in his direction.

"Welcome ta Willowdale," he said. "Make yerselves ta home."

"Will do."

He stepped back a few feet and watched the driver position the van in the center of the lot. When the engine stopped, all three men jumped down from the cab and rushed to the rear door of the van. Each of them wore white coveralls with the business name written on the back, and without a word among them, they started unloading their gear.

"I'm gonna be right over there if ya need me."

He pointed toward the gym and walked over to stand next to the side door. For several minutes, he watched the men perform their well-ordered routine.

"Just let me know if ya need somethin'."

When they didn't answer, it was obvious to him they didn't need his help. Instead of standing there and doing nothing, he went inside the gym and closed the door.

The sound of his footsteps on the wooden floor ricocheted off the concrete block walls as he searched for the electric panel. When he found it, he snapped on the overhead lights.

"Yep," he said. "It's gonna be a good day."

He was glad Mrs. Ivey reserved the gym for the potluck. Even if she didn't know there was still going to be one, he was pretty sure the place was big enough to handle however many people showed up.

Twenty-nine

It was finally July fourth, and I woke up before the alarm went off. Maybe I wasn't going to have a party or gifts or anything, but I was a sixteen-year-old girl with a mission.

"Look out, Mr. Martin," I said. "I'm old enough to get my driver's license."

Even though the dormer window was wide open all night, the tiny bedroom was stifling. It was definitely going to be a hot and humid day.

The only cover on my bed was a light cotton sheet, but it was way too heavy for the warm room. I kicked it off, bounced out of bed and hurried over to the tiny closet.

"Guess I don't have to worry about what to wear today," I said. "I won't be running errands."

I rifled through all my clothes twice. I finally decided on my favorite wrap-around skirt, a sleeveless blouse and a pair of sandals. When I was finished dressing, I hurried downstairs.

Everything appeared to be the same as any other day. Grandma was in her bedroom, humming the same nonsensical tune she always hummed. George was standing beside his food bowl, panting and wagging his tail.

"Good morning, big guy. Are you hungry?"

I didn't know when Grandma would come out of her room. Instead of starting breakfast, I fed George his morning ration of food and refilled his water bowl. There would be plenty of time to fix our own breakfast when Grandma was ready.

The window over the sink was open, and a light breeze blew in. The air was warmer and more humid than when I left my bedroom, but it was still a good day for a birthday.

"It's too nice to work today, George," I said. "Thank goodness, the café is only open for a couple of hours."

Just as I bent down to scratch behind the little pug's ears, Grandma swung her bedroom door open. Instead of her usual work clothes, she wore a light blue sundress and white sandals. Her hair was tied neatly in a bun.

"It's getting late, dear," she said. "We must get to town and be ready when our customers arrive."

"Of course."

My heart sank. As always, her main concern was keeping her customers happy. I guessed she really did forget it was my birthday.

"Why doesn't Irene come in today and make the sandwiches, Grandma?"

"Irene works extremely hard. She deserves to be home on holidays."

I tried to make sense of her logic, but it escaped me. It seemed to me we all deserved to be home on holidays.

"Let's not dawdle, Shirley," she said. "We can get something to eat at the café."

"Yes, Grandma."

George seemed to understand the urgency. He let out a single yip, clicked across the kitchen and stood by the back door. I grabbed his leash and attached it to his collar.

At least you have a good excuse, big guy, I thought. You never did know it was my birthday.

"Are you ready, dear?"

I looked down at George. His tail wagged, and he pulled on his leash.

"It looks as if everybody's ready for work, Grandma."

Without a word, she fit the straw hat on her head and stepped out onto the porch. Before she walked down the steps, she looked over her shoulder at me.

"By the way," she said. "Jimmy will be watching George for us today."

My mouth dropped open at the thought. Why Jim? I hoped, of all days, I would be the one to watch him.

"Isn't the general store closed today?"

"It usually is, but Jimmy told me he's doing inventory all day."

"Then, I'll pick up George after we close the café and bring him home early."

"Not today."

"No?"

"Since Jimmy has to work, I told him to enjoy George the entire day."

It didn't make sense he should stay all day with Jim when I could take him home with me. I really was confused, but like a considerate granddaughter, I held my tongue and didn't argue the point.

Grandma didn't give me a reason for her decision. She just hurried off the steps and picked up her pace. George and I stood on the porch, watching her.

"Well, George, you'll never be able to keep up with her," I said. "But I'm only carrying you until we get to town."

Thirty

"Yes, sir, I'm thinkin' we're ready."

Mr. Martin stood outside the side entrance to the gym and scanned the parking lot. Tiny dust devils whirled around the cars and trucks as their drivers accelerated across the bone-dry gravel.

Tubes of fireworks, neatly lined up in several rows across the center of the lot, were marked off by orange cones to warn people to stay away. Before the pyrotechnic experts went home to get a bite to eat, they promised him they would be back before dark.

"Can't believe we did all this fer that city girl," he said, shaking his head.

Each of the volunteers from Willowdale and the surrounding farms spent a couple of hours getting the gym ready. He knew most everyone who came to help, and he was glad to see they all worked hard.

The men and the older boys set up a dozen folding tables at one end of the gym floor and decorated them with red, white and blue bunting. They arranged the folding chairs in groups of two or three along the walls. When that was done, they took turns sweeping up the gym floor with a push mop they found in the janitor's closet.

The women and the older girls strung a "Happy Birthday" banner across the stage at the other end of the gym. After that, they stacked paper plates, paper napkins, plastic silverware and paper cups on the main table just inside the gym door.

Since a lot of the younger women brought their children along, the youngsters were put to work, too. They took rags and dusted the bleachers that covered half the wall space on both sides of the gym floor.

One of the farmers even brought a grill in the back of his truck and offered to roast Mrs. Ivey's hot dogs. His son, one of the players on the basketball team, rounded up enough ketchup and mustard from their neighbors to serve everyone at least twice.

"Ya'd be real proud if ya could see all this, Aunt Maude."

There wasn't much time before the potluck was scheduled to begin. Everyone was headed home to gather up their families and their food. Judging by the number of volunteers, he figured it would be a huge turnout.

"I'm not thinkin' of it as a party fer Shirley," he said. "No, sir, it's a potluck an' a little birthday mixed in."

He locked the gym door, pulled off his hat and dug a handkerchief out of his pocket. While he wiped away the perspiration from his face and the band inside his hat, he looked up at the sky.

"It's a scorcher, fer sure."

He eased his hat back on and stuffed the handkerchief into his pocket. As he walked toward the old truck, one of the women who organized the food waved at him through her open car window. He waved back and shouted at her.

"Don't ya worry, Margaret. I'm gonna make sure Jimmy gits the hot dogs an' buns from the café."

"Don't you worry, Mr. Martin," she said. "We're all bringing plenty to eat."

She rolled up her window and drove off, followed by a string of other vehicles. Most of the drivers honked at him as they passed by, and he gave each one a quick wave.

"I'm pretty sure Mrs. Ivey won't mind us takin' the hot dogs an' buns," he said to himself. "She already promised ta bring 'em."

Thirty-one

When the three of us got to the café, Grandma went straight to the kitchen. It was too hot to leave George outside, so I took him in with me and tied his leash to the magazine rack. I didn't think she would mind if he stayed there for just a few minutes.

"You be good and don't make a sound, George."

Grandma was busy gathering the sandwich makings, and I didn't think she needed my help. There was something more important I needed to do before I did anything else.

I went behind the lunch counter and searched on all the shelves. It only took a minute to find what I was looking for.

"Here it is, George. Right where Grandpa said it was."

I picked up the wooden box, put it on the counter and carefully opened the lid. Just as he once told me it would be, the American flag was neatly folded and wrapped in white tissue paper.

With great care, I peeled the paper away and lifted the flag from the box. I unfolded it until I found the four metal grommets along its edge.

"You stay here, George. I'll be right back."

As long as I could remember, there was a wooden dowel secured to the bricks beside the front door. I carried the flag out there and slid a grommet over each of the four hooks evenly spaced along the rod.

I brushed out the wrinkles and made sure the cotton material hung straight. When I was satisfied it was perfect, I took a step back.

I had spent so much time feeling sorry for myself about my birthday, I almost forgot about Grandpa's flag. The idea I could be so thoughtless made me sick to my stomach. I wanted to vomit.

The Fourth of July meant so much more to me and my family than a birthday party and presents. Several men in our family had been to war, and two of them had died. It was the one day of the year we set aside time to honor their sacrifices.

"I'm so sorry I almost forgot," I said. "I promise all of you I'll never let that happen."

When my queasy stomach settled down, I went back inside the café. I hurried over to George, untied his leash from the rack and put my arms around his neck.

"I really need a hug right now, big guy."

I hated the thought of leaving him with Jim all day, but I knew I couldn't stall any longer. Without telling Grandma I was leaving, I walked George over to Aunt Maude's general store.

When I opened the door, I was startled to see the place in a complete shambles. There were boxes and cans all over the floor, and paperwork was scattered across the mail counter.

"What a mess, Jim," I said. "I thought the store was closed on holidays."

"Usually it is," he said. "I just thought I'd get some inventorying done today."

"But it's the Fourth of July."

I unhooked the leash from George's collar and watched him wind his way across the cluttered floor. When he found the open door to Aunt Maude's apartment, he disappeared inside without a backward glance.

"Yeah, well," he said. "There's nothing going on today anyway."

I wanted to tell him about my birthday. Maybe if he knew there was something extra special about the day, he'd change his attitude. Instead, I decided to just be nice to him.

"I'm sorry you have to work today."

He turned his back to me and began counting aloud the number of cans in one of the boxes. He was being ruder than normal, so I abandon the nice approach.

"I'll pick up George before you close for the day," I said to his back. "Remember, he goes home with me."

I didn't wait for an answer. I turned around, hurried outside and let the door slam shut.

Across the street, Grandma stood on the sidewalk in front of the café with her apron on and her back toward me. Her fists were resting on her hips, and she was looking up at the flag. I crossed the street and stood next to her.

"Thank you for hanging the flag, dear," she said. "I was afraid it wouldn't get put up this year."

"I'll never let that happen, Grandma."

We studied the flag for a few seconds. Then, we went inside to start our work.

On a table in the center of the dining room, Grandma had piled several loaves of bread. Next to them were jars and jars of peanut butter and jelly.

"Shirley, you are in charge of making the sandwiches, and I will wrap them."

"How many sandwiches would you like me to make?"

"I'm not certain."

"Okay. You tell me when to stop."

I washed my hands, put on a clean apron and lined up two rows of bread slices. I spread peanut butter on one row and slathered grape jelly on the other.

When both rows were complete, I slapped the opposing halves together and sliced each sandwich on the diagonal. One at a time, I handed them to Grandma to wrap in waxed paper.

"That's very efficient, dear."

"Thank you."

After an hour, my hands and the knives were covered with sticky brown and purple, and my back ached from bending over the table. I paused, straightened up and looked over at Grandma.

Her apron was smudged with peanut butter and jelly, and there were several stacks of wrapped sandwiches in front of her. I was sure those were enough, but she tore more waxed paper from the roll.

"Do you think we need so many?" I said.

"We never know how many we'll need, but we want to be prepared."

We took a short break to carry two stacks of sandwiches to the walk-in cooler. Then, it was back to work.

For another hour, I spread and slathered, spread and slathered. I was quickly approaching the point when I never wanted to look at peanut butter and jelly ever again.

"Ah, Grandma, does everybody want peanut butter and jelly?"

"With Irene taking the day off, I'm afraid they don't have a choice."

I put the knife down and wiped my hands on my apron. I moaned a little, stood up straight again and stretched.

"Perhaps you should rest a little while, dear."

"Oh, no, I'm fine."

I bent over the table again and opened a new package of bread. As if I were dealing a deck of cards, I laid out two new rows of slices.

"I just figure if we go faster, we can get done sooner."

I laughed a little at that, but Grandma didn't. She grabbed a sandwich, laid it on a square of waxed paper and folded the paper around it like an envelope.

"We'll work as long as necessary, young lady."

I glanced over at the clock behind the counter. It was already one o'clock. Well past the noon opening.

When I looked outside, I expected to see a line of people waiting to buy their picnic supplies. There wasn't. The only person I saw was Pastor Lawrence pulling up to the front of the café in his drab green sedan.

"Where are all the customers?" I said.

"Perhaps the good pastor is our first one."

We both stopped what we were doing and watched him walk up to the café door. Without a pause, he came inside and joined us at our table.

"Well, Pastor," Grandma said. "How are you on this fine day?"

"Please, call me Albert."

"Albert it is," she said. "You may call me Marie."

He smiled at that, but I could tell he was nervous. He kept wringing his hands and looking down at the floor. I couldn't help noticing he had on the same navy blue slacks and black dress shoes he always wore.

"Pastor Lawrence, would you like a sandwich?"

"No, thank you."

"Well, then," Grandma said. "How may we help you?"

"Well, Marie, I think this is much too nice a day for you two to be inside."

Grandma wiped her hands on her soiled apron and tucked a loose strand of hair back into the bun at her neck. She came around the table and offered the pastor a chair.

"I agree it's a beautiful day, but Shirley and I have too much work to do to enjoy it."

He sat down on the chair Grandma offered, but he didn't relax. He sat up so straight it looked as though he had a broomstick stuck up the back of his shirt.

"Is something wrong, Albert?"

"Actually, I was wondering if you and Shirley would care to take a ride with me and see some of our local scenery."

There went my mouth, dropping open again. I stood there with my hand around the peanut butter jar and stared at him.

"That's very kind of you to offer," she said. "But Shirley and I have several more sandwiches to make before our customers arrive."

I stayed out of the discussion. After all, I was more than a little biased. My duty was to Grandma and her customers, but it was my birthday. Couldn't we just go for a little ride?

"The life of a pastor can be so busy," he said. "It isn't often I find a day to take a break from my duties."

Grandma laid the last wrapped sandwich next to the others and wiped her hands on her apron. I stood beside her, my jelly knife in midair.

"As tempting as it is, I can't leave the café before I serve all my customers."

He looked outside. Then, he glanced around the empty café.

"It appears to me you have enough sandwiches here for everyone."

Both Grandma and I looked out at the deserted street. The only vehicle in sight was the pastor's car, and no one was coming through the door.

"I'm almost certain someone will be here soon."

"Of course, Marie," he said. "I understand."

Grandma studied the stack of sandwiches on the table and glanced around the room. Her face softened a little.

"I suppose we could stop long enough for a cold drink."

"That would be very nice," the pastor said. "But it looks to me as though you could use a longer break than just a cold drink."

Grandma wiped her hands one more time, untied her apron and draped it over the back of a chair. She tucked another loose strand of hair into the bun.

I lowered the jelly knife and watched her. I didn't know what she was thinking, but I hoped my day was going to get a little more interesting.

"I suppose we could take a little time off for a short ride," she said. "But only a short ride, mind you."

"Oh, Grandma, thank you."

I didn't think I could smile any wider. I removed my filthy apron and threw both aprons in with the dirty table rags behind the counter.

"I'll go get each of us a bottle of pop to take along," she said.

While she was in the kitchen, Pastor Lawrence and I gathered the stacks of sandwiches and stored them in the walk-in cooler. Then, we cleared the table of the bread and the peanut butter and jelly jars and put it all in the kitchen.

When everything was put away, Grandma and I took turns cleaning up in the tiny bathroom, and the pastor kept himself busy by scrubbing down the sticky table. It was two o'clock by the time all of us were finished.

"Ye gods and little fishes," Grandma said. "Where did the time go?"

With no potential customers in sight, we each took a bottle of the pop, and Grandma locked up the café. Pastor Lawrence took his place behind the wheel of his car, Grandma sat on the passenger side, and I settled for the back seat.

"Remember, Albert," Grandma said. "We can only take a short ride."

I didn't understand why Grandma was worried about the time. The café was already closed.

"Where are we going?" I said.

The pastor turned in his seat and looked at me. He wore a slight grin.

"Where have you been since you came here for the summer?" he said.

"I haven't been anywhere except Lake Sullivan."

"You leave it to me. This ride should be quite the adventure for you."

As we pulled away from the café, I spotted the "closed" sign in the general store's window. Mr. Spencer's truck was at the end of the block, heading in the opposite direction. Jim was at the wheel with George on his lap.

"Where do you suppose he's going?"

"What did you say, dear?"

Grandma twisted around in the front seat and looked back at me. She looked annoyed. I decided it wasn't a good time to ask any questions.

"It wasn't important, Grandma," I said. "I was just think-ing out loud."

Thirty-two

As we drank our pop, we rode down Main Street and out into the countryside. In a few minutes, we came to a narrow, gravel road that cut through a stand of hardwood trees. Pastor Lawrence slowed his car and turned onto it.

I took the opportunity to turn around and look out the back window. I hoped to see Mr. Spencer's truck, but it was already out of sight.

"This road leads to the town's cemetery, Shirley," the pastor said. "I understand you have several family members there."

I turned back around and tried to pay attention, but I couldn't. I was worried about George and wondered why Jim took him out of the store.

"Shirley, did you hear Albert?"

"I'm sorry. Was it something about the cemetery?"

"That's alright," he said. "You just enjoy the view."

The breeze from the open windows tugged at my pony tail and a few stray wisps of hair whipped around my face. I felt messy, and I tried to hold my hair in place with my free hand. When that didn't work, I gave up the effort. The air felt good on my face, and who cared how my hair looked anyway?

When we got to the cemetery, Pastor Lawrence pulled to a stop near the entrance. We sat there with the engine idling.

"What're we doing?" I said.

"Is everything alright, Albert?"

Instead of answering, the pastor opened his door and stepped out onto the dusty road. He rested his hand on the roof of the car and looked through the back window at me.

"I think it's time you tried your hand at driving."

As usual, my mouth dropped open. I didn't think I heard right.

"What?"

"Albert," Grandma said. "Whatever do you mean?"

"I believe it's time your granddaughter got in a little practice, don't you?"

Grandma was speechless. She looked back at me, then over at the pastor. I could see her mind working.

"Well, I suppose so," she said. "But only for a short ride."

"Oh, Grandma, do you mean it?"

"I think it's time to rethink your grandpa's old rule against women driving," she said, "and break it."

"Really?"

"I don't see how it would hurt just this once."

"Grandma, you really are the best."

I didn't want to give her enough time to have second thoughts. I put my empty pop bottle on the floor and sprang out the back door.

I must have startled Pastor Lawrence. He stepped back a safe distance from the front door and gave me plenty of room to get by him.

I slipped into the driver's seat and closed the door. While I got comfortable and studied the gauges on the dashboard, Grandma moved to the back seat and the pastor sat down on the seat beside me.

"Don't worry about this, Marie," the pastor said. "Everything is legal as long as there's a licensed driver in the front seat with Shirley."

"I wasn't worried about the legality."

I looked at Grandma's reflection in the rearview mirror. She sat directly behind the pastor with her hands folded in her lap and her lips drawn tight.

"It's okay, Grandma," I said. "Mom let me drive her car up and down the driveway at home."

"Up and down the driveway," she said. "That certainly doesn't instill in me a great deal of confidence in this undertaking."

I didn't want her to be any more nervous, so I didn't mention Mom's car had an automatic transmission instead of a manual shift like the pastor's car. But I was eager to learn. If I wanted a license to drive Grandpa's truck, I needed to take full advantage of Pastor Lawrence's offer to teach me.

"Don't worry, Marie," he said. "We'll just take a short ride."

The engine still idled, and I worried we would run out of gas. I checked the fuel gauge. It read half full.

"Now, Shirley, what you need to do is to put your right foot on the brake pedal and your left foot on the clutch pedal."

"Okay."

"Now, move the gear shift toward you and down into first gear."

"Okay."

"Next, you need to keep your left foot on the clutch," he said. "Take your right foot off the brake and put it on the gas pedal."

"Okay."

"Now, here's the tricky part."

"There's a tricky part?" Grandma said.

"Ease your foot off the clutch while you slowly push on the gas pedal."

"Okay."

He was right about it being tricky. As soon as I did as he said, the car lurched forward with a jerk, and the engine died.

"Oops."

"Oh, my word," Grandma said. "This is really quite interesting."

"That's alright," the pastor said. "Try it again, Shirley."

"Okay."

I started the engine according to his instructions, and the second try was much better. The car still jerked, but the engine didn't die. We actually moved forward down the road.

"Now, let's try second gear."

"Okay."

I shifted through all three gears until the car was moving at a breakneck speed of 20 miles an hour. I couldn't have been prouder of myself.

"It's always important to stay on your side of the road, however," he said. "Give oncoming traffic their half."

I took the hint and pulled to the right side of the road. Fortunately, there was no oncoming traffic to worry about. It seemed the whole county heard I was driving and purposely stayed away.

"I'll get better, Grandma," I said, gripping the steering wheel with all my strength. "I just need a little practice."

"Of course you do, dear."

"That's the real difference between growing up in a city and growing up in a small town," the pastor said.

"What do you mean?" I said.

"You don't have the same opportunities to learn to drive," he said. "Here you learn to drive farm equipment almost before you can walk."

He was right. We city girls dreamed of driving when we turned sixteen, but farm girls drove because they had to. I envied them.

"Well, I think you have the basic feel for the car," he said. "Let's go see some country."

"Okay."

Grandma was very quiet in the back seat. Even though I couldn't see her face while I was driving, I could feel the tension. To gain her confidence, I needed to do my absolute best.

Thirty-three

"Are you sure?"

"I'm sure, Dad," Jim said. "I saw Pastor Lawrence and Mrs. Ivey drive out of town."

"And Shirley?"

"She must've been in the backseat."

"And you're sure they didn't see you leave the store?"

"I don't think so."

He helped his father sweep loose pieces of grain off the first floor of the mill while George slept on a blanket next to the open door. The little pug snored softly, and his eye lids twitched.

"Look, Dad," he said. "He feels right at home already."

His father hung his broom on a hook. He turned two wooden crates on their ends and plopped down on the closest one.

"You've been a big help here," his father said. "And at the store, too, when you made Shirley think you didn't care anything about today."

Jim smiled and nodded his head. Making Shirley uncomfortable was what he liked to do best.

"Yeah, Dad," he said. "It was fun watching her get mad because she didn't think I knew it was her birthday."

He sat down on the other crate and raked his hands through his hair. It was hot, and his T-shirt was saturated with sweat.

His father wiped at his forehead with a handkerchief and let out a deep sigh. His face was glistening with perspiration, and from the way he slouched, Jim could see he was exhausted.

"If I didn't know better," his father said, "I'd say there's a storm on the way."

"Not according to Mr. Wilson."

"What did he say?"

"He says his arthritis isn't acting up."

They both sat quietly for several minutes and watched George sleep. A light breeze blew in through the door, but it offered little relief from the heat.

"Does Pastor Lawrence know he's supposed to get Mrs. Ivey and Shirley to the gym by five o'clock, Dad?"

"Mr. Martin said he told him to do just that."

Jim waited for his father to rest a few more minutes. When he thought the time was right, he turned to him and asked the one question that really mattered to him.

"Dad?"

"Yes, Jimmy."

"Have you come up with an idea how we can afford to keep George?"

His father reached out and rested a hand on his shoulder. Since his mother's death, his father had been distant, almost cold. That simple show of affection meant more to him than he realized.

"I haven't thought of anything that makes any sense."

Jim wiped at his teary eyes with the sleeve of his T-shirt and sniffed a little at his own show of emotion. He nodded at his father.

"If I use Mrs. Ivey's truck, I can get a bigger paper route," he said. "That would help a little."

"I know you mean well, but that money is strictly for your college fund."

His father lifted his hand off his shoulder and slouched again. Jim thought he looked more and more tired by the minute.

"But,—"

"No buts, Jimmy. We'll talk about it again tomorrow."

Thirty-four

Once I learned to shift through all three gears and not kill the engine, I drove us all around the countryside. I practiced my start and stop skills and my right and left turns at every intersection. All of my maneuvers led us farther from Willowdale and deeper into the heart of farm country.

"This is fun, Grandma."

"Yes, dear," she said. "But we must get back to work."

"I thought the cafe was closed for the rest of the day."

"I have more business to attend to."

I felt my lower lip slip into its familiar pout. If I sounded pathetic enough, I hoped I would get my own way.

"But, Grandma, I'm just getting the hang of it."

"I warned you we wouldn't have much time, young lady."

I didn't need to look at her to know she was upset. I could hear it in her voice. So, I slid my lip back into its proper place and concentrated on my driving.

"Since we're this far from town," the pastor said, "there's a place I'd like to show both of you."

"And just where would that be exactly?"

"It can't be very far, Marie, and I'm certain both of you will enjoy it."

The car jiggled as Grandma adjusted her position on the back seat. I could just imagine the disapproving look she gave the pastor. The temperature in the car seemed to drop several degrees.

"Grandma?"

From the corner of my eye, I saw the pastor check his watch. I wondered if we were keeping him from something important.

"This shouldn't take more than a few minutes," he said, "and it's on the way back to town."

I didn't say another word and held the steering wheel in a tight grip. I focused my attention on dodging potholes while Grandma mulled over his suggestion.

When she spoke again, it was obvious the pastor's gentle words were more convincing than my ridiculous pout. The temperature in the car rose a little above the freezing mark.

"Ye gods," she said. "It appears I'm out numbered."

"Grandma?"

"As long as it's on the way, I see no reason why we shouldn't see what the pastor wishes to show us."

"Thanks, Grandma."

Inwardly, I was all smiles. Our adventure was getting more interesting, and I couldn't wait to see what Pastor Lawrence had in mind. Besides, I wasn't ready for my first real driving lesson to end.

The rolling hills around us were covered with fields of fledgling crops, and each field looked like one square on a gigantic patchwork quilt. About every mile or so, the pattern was interrupted by acres and acres of dense woods.

Now and then, we passed a farmhouse or a barn, but I never saw a soul at any of them. I didn't know why we had the roads all to ourselves, but it was fun driving on roads that rose and fell with the contour of the land.

"Are these roads always so empty?" I said.

"Not always," the pastor said.

I didn't know what he meant by that, but I imaged it was because of the holiday. It just seemed strange everyone was off the roads at exactly the same time.

The longer I drove, the more comfortable I became. Before long, I felt at ease enough to relax my stranglehold on the steering wheel.

"Isn't it beautiful out here, Grandma?"

"Yes, dear."

I studied the road and every landmark we passed, but I didn't know why I bothered. I didn't have any idea where we were.

"Pastor Lawrence, are we headed in the right direction?"

He scanned the road ahead, then twisted around and studied the road behind us. When he turned forward again, he pointed toward a stand of trees at least two hillsides ahead from us.

"I suppose there ought to be a road back to town over there somewhere."

"Ought to be?" Grandma said.

"I've never been on this particular road before."

I glanced to my right. The pastor was staring straight ahead, his knuckles white from gripping the door handle. When I looked at the rearview mirror, Grandma was staring out the side window, and the temperature in the car dropped a few degrees again.

"Are we lost, Albert?"

"It would be very difficult to get lost, Marie, when all the main roads are designed on a grid system."

"I see."

"Of course, none of these side roads seem to follow that pattern."

"Oh, my."

For several minutes, we drove in silence. Pastor Lawrence searched for a road leading back to town, but I wished my driving lesson would go on forever.

"Wouldn't it be more prudent if we were to stop and consider our next move?"

"You're probably right, Marie," he said. "But let's turn left at the next road and see if I recognize anything."

I could barely keep from giggling. It was my first attempt at driving on real roads, and we were lost. The day couldn't get any better.

"Can my watch be correct?" Grandma said. "Four o'clock?"

The pastor didn't make a comment about the time. He sat quietly and gripped the door handle while I turned the car left at the next road.

At first, the road looked similar to all the others. Its surface was a mixture of dirt and gravel and pocked with scattered potholes. Instead of skirting the trees the way most of the other roads did, however, it cut a path straight through them.

The mixture of trees grew right up to the edge of the road, and their branches arched across from both sides. The longer we drove, the denser they grew, and soon, the sunlight barely penetrated the branches.

I shifted into second gear and slowed the car to practically a crawl. I wanted to enjoy the coolness of the shade and the beauty all around us.

"This is wonderful," I said.

"What do you think, Albert?" Grandma said.

"I think it's very beautiful."

"No," she said. "Do you think this road will take us back to town?"

"It does seem to be headed in that direction."

"Seems to be?"

In another mile or so, the road narrowed at the approach to a one lane bridge. The long wooden span crossed a dry creek bed, but it didn't have a solid driving surface. There were two parallel rows of planks along its full length. Each row of planks was the width of a car tire.

I steered the car to the center of the road, drove up to the edge of the bridge and stopped. I didn't know what to do next.

"Pastor?"

"Just keep your eyes looking forward, Shirley, and drive straight ahead."

I shifted the car into first gear and eased the front tires onto the front edge of the planks. Barely above an idle, I urged the car forward until we reached the center of the span.

I turned toward the pastor. He was staring out the windshield, and his hand was still gripping the door handle.

"What happens if the tires fall off the boards?"

"They won't if you keep your eyes—"

Before the pastor could finish, the left rear tire dropped off its plank. The front of the car twisted to the right. I gripped the wheel with both hands and jammed it to the left.

"Oh, my."

"Hold on, Grandma."

I spun the wheel a full rotation to the right. But the torque between the rear and the front axels was too much for me. The steering wheel jumped from my hands.

"Oh, no."

I threw my hands in the air to stay clear of the free spinning wheel. With everything out of control, the right front tire fell off its plank, and the car came to a stop with a jolt.

I slammed both feet on the brake pedal to make sure we were stopped. My heart pounded, and my hands shook. I couldn't get a full breath.

For a moment, Grandma and the pastor didn't move or say anything. The tension in the car was thicker than Irene's bread pudding.

"Ye gods," Grandma finally said.

I looked over at Pastor Lawrence. I forgot to depress the clutch pedal when I braked. The engine was dead.

"Well, now," he said. "Don't forget the key."

"The key?"

"The key, Shirley. Turn it off."

I switched the key to the off position, took my feet off the brake and leaned against the seat back. Grandma reached over and put her hand on my shoulder.

"I'm sure everything will be fine, dear."

"Oh, Grandma, I'm so sorry."

"I know you are."

Without a word, Pastor Lawrence opened the passenger door and stepped onto the bridge. He began inspecting the situation by walking to the front of the car. All I could see was the frown on his face.

I can't believe how stupid I am, I thought. I just ruined everything.

"Let's see if there's something we can do, Shirley," he said.

My knees were weak, but I managed to get out of the door and walk to the front of the car. It didn't take me long to figure out the problem.

The car rested diagonally across the center of the wooden span. Three of the tires were off the planks, and the front of the car tilted to the right. The situation looked hopeless.

My fears were confirmed when the pastor walked to the back of the car. He bent over and looked through the rear window at Grandma.

"There seems to be only one thing to do," he said.

"And what might that be?"

"Someone has to walk to town for help."

"That seems a bit extreme," she said. "There must be a farm close by where we can use a telephone."

The pastor stood up straight and wiped his hand across his forehead. When he looked at me, I saw something in his eyes other than disgust. I saw disappointment and sadness.

"Even if we could find a farmhouse, there won't be anyone at home to help us."

Thirty-five

Mr. Martin scanned the huge crowd. It looked to him as if the whole county came to the Fourth of July potluck. The dozen tables at the end of the gym were crammed with dishes, and everyone walked around carrying a paper plate covered with food like baked beans, deviled eggs and five-bean salad. He couldn't see an end to the variety of foods the families brought.

Bill Spencer walked up to him and slapped him on the back. He wore a huge smile.

"Well, Mr. Martin," he said. "My boy says you know how to get things done, and he's right."

"I got a lota help from all these folks."

"I was wondering, though. Where's the birthday girl?"

Mr. Martin checked his watch. It was well past five o'clock, and he didn't have any idea what was keeping the three of them. Pastor Lawrence promised him they'd get to the gym no later than five.

"The pastor took 'em fer a little ride in his car, ya know."

"Yeah, I know."

"He mighta let Shirley drive."

"He might have?"

"That's the plan."

"You and the pastor had a plan?"

"We figured givin' her a drivin' lesson was a good way ta keep her an' Mrs. Ivey outa our hair fer a while."

"But shouldn't they be here by now?"

"She's a city girl, ya know. Maybe she's a slow learner."

Bill started to say something, but he stopped when his son walked up to them. Jimmy was carrying a paper plate loaded with chocolate brownies.

"These aren't as good as Aunt Maude's cookies, but they're pretty good."

Each of them took a couple of the brownies, and they looked around the room as they ate. The high school dance band was on the stage tuning up their instruments, and Bob McNary was testing the microphone.

With so much noise on stage, the volume of the conversations around the gym was deafening. Bill shouted to be heard.

"You don't suppose they had a problem, do you?"

Mr. Martin pointed to his ear and shook his head. He couldn't hear anything in all the commotion.

"Let's git outa here so we don't have ta yell."

He stuffed his mouth with his last bite of brownie, put one hand on Bill's arm and the other hand on Jimmy's shoulder. The three of them snaked their way around the noisy crowd and out the door.

The parking lot near the gym was chaos. A long line of parents stretched beyond the truck with the barbeque grill. They waited for Mrs. Ivey's hot dogs while their young children screamed and chased each other around parked cars.

Just beyond the barbeque truck, a net was strung between a tree and the corner of the fireworks van. A dozen and a half of the older boys were playing a rowdy game of volleyball.

Instead of staying there to talk, he led Bill and Jimmy toward the center of the parking lot. He didn't stop until he reached one of the orange cones marking a row of fireworks.

"Don't know what's goin' on," he said. "But I'm thinkin' it's best ta go lookin' fer 'em."

Just then, a white flash lit up the sky to the west where a bank of black clouds was building. A distant rumble of thunder followed, and the air filled with the odor of ozone.

"Oh, no," Jimmy said.

"Looks like it's gonna be a bad one."

"We need to get all the men with trucks," Bill said, "and start combing the roads for them."

"You an' Jimmy go on ahead."

He knew how serious a thunderstorm could be, but it didn't do any good to stand there and worry. He needed to help, too.

"Don't ya fret about us back here," he said. "We'll git these folks inside an' git that equipment covered up."

Bill nodded at him, and he and his son raced toward the gym. Three men in white coveralls stopped, wide-eyed, when they saw the two running toward them.

"Better get those fireworks covered," Bill said without stopping. "A storm is coming."

Thirty-six

With Pastor Lawrence in the lead and Grandma ahead of me, we eased around the car and along the nearest plank in a single file. We were careful not to lose our balance and step off the narrow piece of lumber. We didn't want to risk falling through the bottom of the bridge to the dry creek bed several feet below.

"I still think I should be the one to walk to town," I said.

"I refuse to wait here," Grandma said. "I must get back to the café."

"But it's my fault."

"Does it help matters to assign blame?"

"No, I guess not."

I stole a backward glance at the abandoned car. From that angle it was easy to see how bad the situation really was.

Both rear tires were off their planks. The left front tire was still on its plank, but the right front tire poked halfway through the bottom of the structure.

Thanks to me, all future traffic was blocked from traveling on the one lane bridge. Grandma was right. Blaming me wouldn't solve the problem.

Pastor Lawrence never looked back at his car, and he walked ahead of us without speaking. I could only image what he was thinking.

When we got to the end of the bridge and stepped onto the road, we continued to follow him in a single file. Still, no one spoke for several more minutes. It was Grandma who finally broke the silence.

"How far do you think we are from town, Albert?"

"I don't know for certain, but it could be a very long walk."

"Oh, my."

"I'm really, really sorry, Grandma."

Her chin jutted upward, and she stumbled a little. I stepped forward and stopped her fall by grabbing hold of her arm.

"I know you're sorry, Shirley," she said. "I don't want to hear any more about it."

She shook my hand off her arm and stepped out in front of me again. We tried to keep up with the pastor, but we lagged farther and farther behind. Open toed sandals were definitely the wrong kind of shoes for a hike on a gravel and dirt country road.

"Pastor Lawrence, could you slow down a little?"

"Yes, Albert. We're not able to keep up with you."

He stopped and waited for us while we picked our way around the potholes. When we finally caught up to him, he was scanning the woods on the left side of the road.

"I have an idea," he said. "If I'm right, I may know a shortcut to town."

224

"You mean we're not lost?"

"Ye gods. Anything would be preferable to walking any longer than necessary in these sandals."

"Well," he said. "I've been calculating the direction of our drive."

"Yes?"

"I suggest we cut across this section of woods."

"Why would we do that?"

"If I'm right, Marie, we'll pop out on the other side and into the next field."

"What in the world would that gain us?"

"Well, from that field we should be able to see the Willowdale water tower."

The trees were so dense, it was impossible to see how far across the woods stretched. I hoped the pastor's calculations were right.

"That could still be miles away from here, couldn't it?" Grandma said.

"I know it isn't a perfect plan, but we might get back to town a little sooner."

He looked at Grandma, then at me. I felt so awful about his car I couldn't look him in the eye. All I wanted to do was sink into the ground and disappear.

"If we don't get back to town soon, my plans will be ruined, Albert."

I didn't understand what she meant. What plans? Couldn't her customers get by without their sandwiches just this once?

She yanked her lace handkerchief out from under the tie at her waist and waved it back and forth in front of her face. The beads of perspiration dotting her upper lip reminded me of the way Aunt Maude looked the night she got sick.

"Are you alright, Grandma?"

"It's nothing," she said with a wave of her hand.

"Maybe we should stop here for a while," I said. "It would give all of us time to rest."

"Don't you treat me as though I'm a child, young lady," she said. "I must get back to the café as quickly as possible."

Oh, boy. First, I got the pastor's car stuck on the bridge. Then, I made Grandma mad. I didn't see how the day could get any worse.

"Happy birthday to me," I said under my breath.

Thirty-seven

"Are we ready?" the pastor said.

I looked at Grandma, and she looked at me. We both nodded at him.

"Well, then, here we go."

Without hesitation, he plunged into the trees on the left side of the road. He seemed confident, and since Grandma and I didn't know what else to do, we plunged in right behind him.

With the pastor in the lead, the three of us walked single file along a faint animal trail that wandered around the trees. Most of the trail was overgrown with brush. It snagged our clothes and scratched our bare skin.

The pastor looked back to check on us once in a while, but he never said a word. It really didn't matter. I was so busy dodging the undergrowth and keeping an eye on Grandma, I didn't have time to talk.

After several more minutes, the pastor stopped beside the trunk of an enormous maple. The tree's foliage blocked so much sunlight, no vegetation grew below it.

"How are you two doing?" he said.

Grandma and I stopped a few feet from him and took a few deep breaths. The ground there was level and soft under our feet.

"I think we should rest here for a moment," Grandma said.

My mouth was dry, my feet hurt, and my legs were scratched. I wasn't going to argue with taking a rest. But I made a mental note to never walk in the woods in a skirt and sandals ever again.

"I think you're right, Marie," the pastor said. "We could use a little rest."

With my hand under her arm, I helped Grandma to the ground about a yard or so from the tree, and I collapsed right beside her. I was too tired to care about the ground's musty smell or to worry about what slimy creatures lived among the moldering leaves.

Pastor Lawrence sat down right next to the tree and leaned his back against the trunk. His shirt was soaked with perspiration, and his navy blue pants were torn in several places.

"This is a much wider span of woods than I thought it would be," he said.

"It does seem to go on forever, Albert."

Her face was a little red, but the beads of perspiration on her upper lip were gone. Nearly half the hair from the bun at her neck was hanging loose.

"How are you feeling, Grandma?"

"You needn't worry yourself about me," she said, licking at her lips. "I just wish I'd brought my bottle of pop with me."

"I think we could all use some water right now," the pastor said.

As if on cue, I heard a deep rumble. The sound was faint, but unmistakable. It was thunder.

"Did you hear that, Grandma?"

"I did, indeed."

The pastor jumped to his feet and brushed off bits of leaves from the seat of his pants. He stepped out from under the tree and looked up.

"Ladies," he said. "I believe we should be on our way."

I looked up at the little slice of sky I could see. Even though it was still bright blue, the sound of thunder left little doubt. A storm was headed our way, and we didn't have any time to waste.

Thirty-eight

Bill gathered all the men who drove trucks to the potluck and assigned each one a different section of the county to search. Even with the best of plans, finding the pastor and Mrs. Ivey and her granddaughter wouldn't be easy. No one knew which direction they took, and the county was riddled with unmapped dirt roads.

"What do you think, Dad?"

"I think we need to find them before that storm hits."

For more than an hour, he and his son Jimmy drove up and down the roads, watching for their friends and keeping an eye on the storm. The ominous cloud on the horizon had ballooned into a thunderhead, and every flash of lightning was followed by a loud clap of thunder.

"The storm is getting awfully close, Dad."

"I know, Jimmy. Pretty soon it'll be too dangerous to be out here looking for them."

His son turned in his seat and looked at him. He took his baseball cap off his head and raked his fingers through his hair.

"But we can't just leave them out here alone."

"I'm afraid we might not have a choice."

He reached over and gave his son's shoulder a squeeze. Then, he dropped his hand onto the back of the pug asleep between them. He gave the little dog a few gentle strokes.

"Thanks for stopping to pick up George, Dad. I hated taking him back to Aunt Maude's store this afternoon."

"It's like I told you, Jimmy. That many people and that much noise would have scared him."

"But being alone in a thunderstorm would have scared him, too."

"Well, he's with us now, and he's safe."

With a big yawn, George rolled onto his back. He stretched out his hind legs until he occupied the entire center section of the seat and fell back to sleep.

For several more minutes, they followed the last dirt road in their section of the search area. They found nothing. Not a sign of the pastor's car or anyone on foot.

If the three weren't found soon, Bill knew he and his son would have to abandon their search. They would need to find shelter in the gym and check in with the other search parties.

"Dad, stop the truck!"

Bill slammed his foot on the brake and grabbed George from flying off the seat. The truck stuttered to a stop.

"What is it, Jimmy?"

His son jammed his cap back on his head. Using his arms for leverage, he thrust his body halfway out the open window and scanned the side of the road.

"Back there," he said. "I think I see something."

A wide-eyed George jumped up and watched him hanging out the window. With his tongue hanging from his mouth, the little dog panted as if he were ready for a new adventure.

Bill threw the truck into reverse and eased backwards along the road. He waited for his son's signal.

"There, Dad!"

When he stopped the truck, Bill looked out the passenger window. He immediately saw what caught his son's attention. A lace handkerchief was stretched across the top of a wild rose bush.

His son leaped out of the truck, grabbed the handkerchief and ran it over to him. Bill turned it over in his hands and put it to his nose.

"No doubt about it," he said. "Only one person in this whole county carries these fancy things with lavender perfume on them."

"Mrs. Ivey."

"That's right."

They smiled at each other, and George wagged his tail until his whole body moved back and forth. He yipped, spun in a tight circle and yipped again.

But their celebration was short-lived. Another volley of thunder rolled over them.

"What do you think we should do, Dad?"

"If she lost this while they were walking, it means they aren't with the pastor's car anymore."

"Why would they leave the car and start walking?"

"I can't answer that one," Bill said, "but I'd sure like to know why they didn't stay on the road."

He pulled the truck over and rolled up the windows. Once he switched off the engine, his son pulled open the passenger door, picked George up off the seat and tucked him under his arm.

"Do you really think it's a good idea to take him out in this weather?"

"Maybe not, Dad, but I figure Mrs. Ivey and Shirley might need to see a friendly face right about now."

Thirty-nine

After our short rest, we continued to follow the pastor along the animal trail and fight our way through heavy brush. As tired as I was, the cool shade in the woods was a welcome relief from the hot, sticky air in the car.

Besides the overwhelming odor of mold from the rotting leaves, I smelled ozone. I looked up at the sky. The blue was gone, and a thin layer of clouds blocked out most of the sunlight. The storm was getting closer.

"Are you certain you know where we're headed?" Grandma said.

"Not exactly," the pastor said. "But I think we're generally headed in the right direction."

"Oh, my."

After we walked another few yards, the ground began a long, gradual climb before leveling off again. That's when Grandma stopped short, and I nearly bumped into her.

"What is it, Grandma?"

"I'm afraid we may have a problem."

I stepped around her. In front of us was a wide ravine filled with stagnant water. Blue-green algae covered the surface and threw off a nose-stinging stench.

"I think you're right," I said.

The pastor stood beside the water, pinching his nose closed against the horrible smell. After a few seconds, he dropped his hand and paced some of the pool's length. He finally returned to where he left Grandma and me waiting.

"Well, now," he said. "I didn't expect this."

I looked up and down the ravine. The brackish water extended in both directions for as far as I could see. Here and there, a few large boulders jutted above its surface.

"What do we do now?" I said.

"We go across right here."

"Oh, my."

"Grab my hand, Marie," he said. "I'll keep you from slipping."

He took her hand, and they went across, balancing their weight from one boulder to the next. I followed behind them with my arms outstretched, careful to step on the same boulders they did. A tightrope walker would have been proud.

At the far side of the ravine, we jumped, one at a time, onto a narrow bank barely wide enough to hold the three of us. It was nestled against the foot of a sharp rise covered with immature birch trees.

"Now what, Pastor?"

"Up there," he said and pointed to the top of the hill.

"Ye gods."

By my estimate, it was only about fifty feet to the top, but it seemed more like a thousand. Climbing up something that steep with slippery leaves under foot would be hard for anyone. I couldn't imagine Grandma being able to manage it.

"I hate to be the one to remind you," the pastor said, "but we need to keep moving."

Grandma gave me one last look, hiked the hem of her dress up to her knees and grabbed hold of the first tree branch. I admired her tenacity.

"Just follow my lead," the pastor said. "And don't look down."

Using the lowest branches, we did as he said and pulled ourselves up the steep incline a little at a time. Grandma paused several times to rest, but we all made it to the top. I was so proud of her I threw my arms around her neck and gave her a huge hug.

"You're the greatest, Grandma."

"My, that was—interesting, wasn't it?"

The pastor and I laughed at her enormous understatement. Without another word, we all collapsed on the ground right where we stood.

We were seated in tall grass at the edge of a large meadow. It was surrounded by mature trees of every kind including a stately sycamore. The whole scene was breathtaking.

"Do you hear that?" I said.

Somewhere in front of us, I heard gurgling water, but I couldn't see anything from where we were sitting. The pastor and I stood up to look across the meadow for the source.

"There it is," he said.

I helped Grandma to her feet, and the three of us pushed our way through the lush grass. On the other side of the meadow, a tall limestone formation jutted upward at a slightly tilted angle. A stream of water oozed from a narrow fissure at its top and plunged into a pool of clear water at its base.

"Wow."

"My gracious."

"Do you think it's safe to drink?" the pastor said.

I didn't wait for an answer. I pushed past them to reach the water first and cupped my hands under the stream. While I gulped the cool water, the overflow ran down my arms and dripped onto my skirt.

After a few swallows, I stepped back so Grandma could get a drink. She tried to keep her clothes dry by putting her mouth directly under the stream and sipping the water. All she got for her efforts was a wet face and water running down her neck and the front of her dress.

"Oh, dear," she said. "There really is an art to this, isn't there?"

She reached for the tie at the waist of her dress, searching for something. She had a puzzled look.

"I think I lost my hankie on the path somewhere," she said. "That was very careless of me."

Without hesitation, she wiped away most of the water from her face with her hands. I could see she felt much better by the grin she wore.

When Pastor Lawrence had his fill of water, he checked his watch again. He looked at us and shook his head.

"This water was a godsend," he said. "But we really must move on."

"Can't we stay here a little longer?" I said.

"It's already six o'clock, and I'm afraid we're still a long way from town."

"Please, Grandma."

"Now, Shirley, you heard what Albert said."

I tried my pout routine and even teared up a little, but my efforts were met with stern looks from both of them. After all, I wasn't a little girl anymore. I was sixteen.

"We can't stay today," Grandma said. "Maybe Albert will drive us here again before the summer is over."

"Really?" I said. "This is the neatest place I've ever seen."

"Yes, indeed, it is—neat."

"We could bring some of your sandwiches and have a real picnic."

"We could, indeed," she said. "But next time we'll wear proper shoes and clothing."

Pastor Lawrence didn't seem excited about the prospect of a future picnic. He kept looking at his watch, at the sky and around the perimeter of the meadow.

"What is it, Albert?"

"We need to decide which way to go from here," he said.

Grandma looked as confused as I felt. I thought he knew which way to go, and I trusted him to get us home safely. I was wrong.

"I guess we really are lost, Grandma."

Forty

I wanted to keep walking in the same direction we were going when we found the meadow. Grandma and Pastor Lawrence wanted to retrace our steps and find an alternate route out of the ravine. We took a vote. I lost.

So, there we stood on the ridge, looking down at the foul water we already struggled to cross. From that vantage point, the hill looked a lot steeper to me than it did when we climbed up.

"Don't either of you worry," the pastor said. "I'll go first."

He turned to face into the slope and was about to begin his descent. The plan was to use the same technique we used to climb up, only in reverse. Instead of pulling ourselves up with the branches, we would use them to stop ourselves from falling. The pastor would lead us down, Grandma would follow him, and I would bring up the rear.

"Remember," he said. "Don't look down."

Just as he was searching for the first branch to grab, I heard a muffled noise I couldn't identify. I reached over and touched Grandma's arm.

"What is it, dear?"

"I think there's something down there."

Pastor Lawrence stopped before he took his first step, and we all stayed very still, listening. Something moved among the trees beyond the ravine, rustling the underbrush.

"Are there bears around here?" I said.

"Not many," the pastor said.

That didn't make me feel any better about our situation. To me, one bear was too many.

"Grandma?"

"Don't worry, dear," she said. "Black bears aren't usually aggressive."

"Should that make me feel better?"

I watched the trees and waited for a hairy, four-legged brute to charge through. If one did, I didn't know what any of us would do. Immature trees weren't strong enough to climb, and I certainly wasn't a very good runner.

The rustling grew louder, and my eyes were fixed on the line of trees. Before I could see the source of the sound, I heard a voice.

"Mrs. Ivey, do you hear me?"

"What in the world?"

"If I didn't know better, I'd say it sounds a lot like Jimmy Spencer," the pastor said.

Before we had a chance to answer the shout, a dog yipped. It was a constant yip, not really a bark, and I knew it could only come from one dog.

"George" I said. "Is that you?"

On the other side of the ravine, Jim burst through the trees at full speed. He stopped at the edge of the stagnant water and looked up at us. George was nowhere in sight.

"So, there you all are."

He was out of breath, and his jeans were covered with bits of branches and a few wild roses. No matter how tired or how dirty he looked, I had to admit he was a welcome sight.

"Hello, Jimmy," the pastor said.

Grandma waved at him. Then, she clapped her hands and bounced up and down.

"You found us," she said.

"Dad's here, too," he said. "He's behind me somewhere."

"And George?" I said.

"He's coming."

Our conversation was easygoing. We sounded more like friends visiting over a backyard fence than standing in the middle of nowhere on a rescue mission with a thunderstorm threatening.

"Why are you up there, Mrs. Ivey?"

"We were hoping to find a shortcut back to Willowdale."

While they talked, George appeared out of the trees. He walked straight toward the filthy water, but Jim put his hand down to stop the little pug's forward momentum.

"Whoa," he said. "You don't want to go in there."

George stopped immediately. He looked tired. His chest heaved, and his tongue hung out the side of his mouth.

"What are you doing here?" I said. "How did you know we needed help?"

"When you didn't show up at the gym when you were supposed to, half the county went searching for you."

I looked at Grandma, and she looked at me. I had no idea what he was talking about, but I suspected she might.

"Show up at the gym, Grandma?"

"There seems to be more to this story than even I know," she said. "Is that right, Albert?"

The pastor's face was bright red, and it wasn't from physical exertion. It was obvious to me he was keeping something from Grandma.

"Do you know what this is all about, Jim?" I said.

"Me and everybody else in the county."

"Never mind that," Grandma said. "How did you find us?"

"We found your handkerchief beside the road."

Grandma put her hand to her waist and laughed. She saw something funny in all the confusion, but I didn't. I was completely lost and didn't see the humor in any of it.

Jim reached down and gave George a pat on his head. The little pug looked up at him and wagged.

"You stay here, George."

"What are you doing?" I said.

"I'm coming over there to help you get down."

Before I could tell him which of the boulders was safe to walk on, he placed a foot on the closest one. When he put his full weight on it, his foot slipped a little on a patch of algae. His arms flailed as he struggled to regain his balance.

"Careful," I said. "They're really slippery."

"Yeah, I noticed."

244

He slowly stepped from one algae covered boulder to the next. He made good progress until he reached the halfway point. When he took his eyes off the putrid water to look up at us, his right foot slipped out from under him.

"Uh, oh," he said.

"Jim?"

He flailed his arms again and reached for the branch of a willow that stretched over the flooded ravine. At first, it looked as though he might have a good grasp on it and regain his balance. But he didn't, and he couldn't.

When his fingers slipped off the branch, there was nothing to stop him. He landed with a splash in the scummy water and disappeared below the surface.

"Ye gods."

"Jimmy?"

"Oh, no," I said.

He was a strong swimmer, and I wasn't concerned he would drown. I was worried George would go into the water after him.

"You stay right there, big guy."

When Jim surfaced, he spit out a mouthful of green water. His hair was coated with the blue-green algae, and his shirt was covered in yellow fuzzy stuff I couldn't identify.

"Yuck," he said. "That's nasty."

"Oh, boy."

"Oh, my."

"Stay right there, Jimmy," Pastor Lawrence said. "I'm on my way."

The rancid water was up to Jim's chest, and he wiped at his eyes with his dirty hands. On the bank, George spun in a tight circle and yipped at him. Then, he yipped again and again and again.

"Don't worry," I said. "Jim's okay."

"Yeah," he said. "I'm just—fine."

When George heard Jim's voice, he stopped spinning and yipping. He stood quietly on the bank and stared at him.

"That's a good boy," Jim said. "You stay right there."

As the pastor eased himself over the edge of the steep rise, he reached for one of the low tree branches. It was too far from his hand.

When he tried to reach for another branch, the smooth soles on his dress shoes slipped on a patch of moldy leaves. Both of his feet went out from under him. Without a branch to stop him, he slid down the hill on his back, ricocheting off saplings and low bushes.

Halfway to the narrow ledge below, his rib cage caught one of the larger trees. He threw his arms around the trunk and scrabbled his feet in the loose leaves. He found footing on a small patch of bare earth beneath the leaves and fell onto his stomach at the base of the tree. For several seconds, he lay there without speaking.

"Oh, no."

"Pastor Lawrence!"

"Albert," Grandma said. "You must be more careful."

Grandma was good at understating the obvious, but I agreed with her sentiment. We didn't need anyone getting hurt.

The pastor's voice sounded a little pained when he spoke. I could see he was struggling to get a breath.

"I promise—I'll be—more careful."

After a few seconds, he released one hand from the tree and rubbed where the trunk connected with his ribs. Then, he got to his knees, grabbed a low branch and pulled himself to his feet. Using one branch after another, he eased himself the rest of the way down the hill until he was safely on the ground.

"Are you okay, Pastor?" Jim said.

"I'll be fine," he said. "Let's get you out of there."

"I'm ready."

He tried several times to get Jim out of the water, but every attempt failed. Either their hands slipped apart when the pastor tried to hoist Jim onto a boulder, or the wet soles on Jim's shoes couldn't find purchase.

"That's okay, Pastor," Jim said. "I'll just walk out."

"Alright," he said. "I'll go back for the women."

As Pastor Lawrence made his way back across the boulders, Jim pushed his way to the other side of the ravine. It was hard to watch. I felt sorry for him having to endure so much filth.

When he finally reached the other side, he pulled himself onto the bank and flopped down. The smell coming off of him must have been awful because George refused to get close.

"Is it that bad?" he said.

"Yip."

While Grandma and I waited for the pastor's help, there was more rustling in the underbrush behind Jim. I thought it might truly be a bear, and I worried about what would happen to George.

I sighed with relief when Mr. Spencer shoved his way through the trees. We didn't need to plan our escape after all.

"Well, what've we got here?" he said.

We must have been quite a site. Jim was flopped on his back and covered in algae and yellow slime, Pastor Lawrence was scrambled halfway up the steep slope, and Grandma and I were perched on the ridge like a couple of birds.

"Dad," Jim said. "I got a little wet."

"I see that."

George looked up at Mr. Spencer and yipped a few times. I think he wanted to tell his side of the story, but a clap of thunder and the first drops of rain interrupted him.

"Well, George," Mr. Spencer said. "Let's get these folks out of here."

Forty-one

Once Pastor Lawrence escorted Grandma and me off the hill and across the ravine, Jim and his father led all of us out of the woods. Halfway into our walk, the few rain drops turned into a downpour, and we were thoroughly soaked by the time we reached the truck.

Grandma and the pastor rode inside the cab with Mr. Spencer. The heater fan blew full blast.

Jim and George and I piled into the bed of the truck. There was a canvas tarp back there, and the three of us huddled underneath it. Not to stay warm, but to stay out of the wind and the pelting rain.

"Well," Jim said. "At least I don't have as much gunk on me anymore."

"Uh-huh."

"What do you mean by that?"

"It's a start," I said. "Your clothes are just a little smelly."

"At least George likes me."

"Are you sure about that?"

The little pug leaned against my legs and looked up at me with his big, round eyes. I lifted him onto my lap, and he snuggled against my chest. I wrapped my arms around him to warm up his trembling body.

Not only was it wet and cold in the back of the truck, but it was noisy, too. All the way back to Willowdale, Mr. Spencer beeped the horn in groups of three blasts, alerting the other searchers we were found.

"I still don't understand what Pastor Lawrence knows that Grandma doesn't, and I have no idea about."

"What?"

"You know what I mean," I said. "Back in the woods you said you knew all about it."

"Well—"

"Well?"

Jim reached over and gave George a light pat on the head. Then, he twisted around so he could look straight at me.

"It all started the day you got here."

"To Willowdale?"

"Yep."

"Okay."

For the rest of the ride, Jim filled me in on the surprise birthday potluck at the gym. I couldn't believe how everyone pulled together to make the day special for me.

"Sorry you didn't get to be there," he said. "I had a great time until we had to go look for you."

"And we know how well that went."

"You just have to rub it in, don't you?"

He squirmed a little and shifted his position. I held onto the tarp until he was finished.

"Was there a birthday cake?"

"Not exactly," he said. "There were birthday brownies."

When George's shivering slowed to only intermittent shaking, I knew he was feeling warmer. I eased his head onto my lap and stroked his wet coat. He curled into a ball, tucked his nose under his back legs and fell asleep.

"Wish I could have been there."

"Yeah," Jim said. "But the day isn't over yet."

"What does that mean?"

"You'll see soon enough."

Sometime during our ride, the storm moved away, and the pounding rain dwindled to a spattering of large drops. For the rest of the ride, Jim and I stayed under the canvas and kept George calm and asleep.

I wanted to go home, change into something dry and use a big, fluffy towel on George. Unfortunately, Mr. Spencer had different ideas.

When the truck stopped, we threw off the canvas and found ourselves parked in front of Grandma's café. All the parking spaces up and down the street were filled with cars and trucks. I couldn't imagine why so many people were in town.

Once we managed to get George and all five of us out of the truck, we paraded single file through the front door of the café. George was so exhausted he was asleep in my arms.

"You sure you don't want me to carry him for you?" Jim said.

"I'm absolutely sure."

All of us were soaked and smelled of leaf mold, but Grandma seemed to have fared the worst. Her cotton sundress hung limp, her legs were covered in scratches and her leather sandals were waterlogged. The hair that once was in a bun at the nape of her neck now hung straight down her back.

My own clothes and sandals were ruined, but I didn't care. My first concern was George.

The café was packed with the searchers, and the walls practically vibrated from the sound of their voices. In fact, it was so noisy I had to shout in order for Grandma to hear me.

"It's a good thing we made all those sandwiches."

"It certainly is, dear."

Several men at the counter were practically inhaling them, and Dr. Thompson was serving more of the sandwiches to people seated at the tables. Miss Spitz followed behind him with a tray loaded with cups of coffee and hot chocolate.

Mrs. Van Berkel appeared from somewhere near the magazine rack and came toward us. Her face was twisted in a maze of worry lines.

"Oh, you poor dears."

She handed Grandma a clean table rag, and Grandma used it to wipe her face and the tips of her hair where the water still dripped. She tried offering a rag to me, too, but I didn't want one. I was busy looking around the room for a place to put George before my arms collapsed.

"Shirley," Jim said. "Over here."

He stood beside the front table, waving for me to join him. Someone had put a canvas jacket on the floor so its plaid flannel lining was on top.

"Perfect," I said.

When George was all settled on top of the jacket, Mr. Wilson and his son Clyde stepped up to Jim and me. Their arms were piled with neatly folded clothes.

"I know they're not much," Mr. Wilson said. "But they're clean and dry."

I was speechless. There stood a man and his son who struggled every day to keep their farm going, and they offered us probably the only other clothes they owned.

"Thank you, Mr. Wilson," I said.

Jim and I separated the stack into sets of one shirt and one pair of pants each. There were just enough sets for all five of us.

While everyone else in the café ate sandwiches, Jim and his father and Pastor Lawrence changed their clothes in the storeroom. Grandma and I took turns using the tiny bathroom to change out of our wet things.

The first thing I did was use my fingers to comb my wet hair into a new pony tail. The shirt was so big I had to roll up the sleeves, and the pants didn't fit any better. I turned the legs up far enough so I wouldn't trip on them. Finally, I decided to go barefoot instead of putting my soggy sandals back on.

I waited near the kitchen door while Grandma finished changing. When she came out of the bathroom, we stood back and inspected each other's outfit. Our plaid flannel shirts and khaki pants hung on us, miles too big. But we were warm and dry and barefoot. It was a wonderful feeling.

"My, we do look stylish, Grandma."

"We do, indeed, my dear."

When we went back to the dining room, Jim and his father and Pastor Lawrence were in their borrowed clothes and seated at the front table. There were sandwiches stacked on a platter and cups of coffee and hot chocolate next to it.

After we sat down, Grandma took a cup of the coffee, and I picked up a cup of the hot chocolate. When I took a sip, the rising steam warmed my face.

"Oh, Grandma," I said. "This is the best birthday I've ever had."

She laughed, and there was a sparkle in her eyes. At that moment, I thought she looked more like a young school girl than my grandmother.

In the chair across from me, Jim smacked his lips and downed his second sandwich. Even with the sleeves on his borrowed shirt rolled up, he managed to get peanut butter on them.

He finally looked up from the food long enough to meet my eyes, and I felt my cheeks turn red. I had to admit he wasn't such a bad person. After all, he did try to be the hero at the ravine.

"I know I look stupid," he said. "But at least I'm not a filthy mess anymore."

"I thought you looked kind of cute in all that icky green stuff."

"Yeah, right," he said and grabbed another sandwich.

Mr. Martin walked over to our table and stood beside Grandma. His old felt hat was in his hands.

"Sorry, Mrs. Ivey," he said. "We ate up all yer hot dogs."

"Don't be concerned about that," she said. "They were my contribution to the potluck, remember?"

"Yes, ma'am."

"I'm just curious how you managed everything without me knowing about it," she said. "I told everyone to forget the potluck since Maude couldn't be there."

"Yeah, but none of us paid any mind."

Mr. Martin kneaded the brim of his hat. He shuffled his feet a little and cleared his throat.

"Aunt Maude said I was right ta go ahead with it anyways."

"I see."

"So it'd be a surprise fer you an' Shirley."

"Oh, it's a surprise alright."

"Yes, ma'am."

He stayed beside Grandma and continued to knead his hat. It looked as though he had something else on his mind.

"I took Robert's flag down when it got dark," he said. "It's back under the counter."

"That was very thoughtful of you."

I was relieved Grandpa's flag was safe and back in its proper place. I smiled at Mr. Martin, but he never looked in my direction.

Just in case he heard me, I said, "Thank you."

I didn't know what else to do, so I handed the platter of sandwiches to Grandma. She offered them to him, but he didn't take one. Instead, he fit his old hat on his head and faded into the crowd at the back of the room.

Grandma scooted her chair a little closer to mine. Her expression turned serious.

"I would like it very much if you would come again next summer.

"You want me to come again?"

"Of course," she said. "But next time, you'll do all the driving for me."

Jim laughed a little too hard at that, but I ignored him. Grandma was paying me a huge compliment.

"What about Mr. Martin?" I said.

"He told me he can't see well enough to drive anymore."

"Everybody's been dodging him on the roads forever," Jim said. "Even turning the streetlights on early didn't help him after a while."

Well, that cleared up the mystery about the lights. The town had worked together to help Mr. Martin for as long as possible.

"But there won't be a surprise potluck," she said. "Not even if Maude writes me another note and pleads with me."

"That's what was in her note?"

"Yes," she said. "Unfortunately, my determination to ignore her and stop the potluck almost ruined the day for everyone."

"But it didn't," I said. "Jim said everything turned out just fine."

"It's all thanks to the hard work of everyone in the county," Grandma said. "They're the ones who made the potluck possible."

I glanced around the noisy dining room at all the people who searched for us. I didn't recognize most of them.

Some were huddled in small groups, talking and laughing. Others sat quietly and ate sandwiches. All the while, Miss Spitz circled the room with the percolator and poured one cup of coffee after another.

"These are very special people, Grandma."

"Yes, they are, dear."

I had spent most of the summer convinced I wouldn't have any fun or find any friends in Willowdale. I was wrong, and I wanted to thank everyone for welcoming me. I just needed to think of the best way to do it.

Grandma laughed at something Jim said, and I looked at her beautiful smile. The potluck at the gym would have been fun, but the impromptu gathering at the café was better than anything anyone could have planned.

"Well," Grandma said. "We have certainly had quite a day."

She stood up and walked to the front window. I walked over to her, and we surveyed the cars and trucks parked outside. I was surprised to see Pastor Lawrence's car parked right next to Mr. Spencer's truck.

"How did your car get here, Pastor?" I said. "I thought it would be stuck on the bridge forever."

The pastor got up from the table and joined us at the window. Something in his manner told me I still had a lot to learn about Willowdale.

"Never underestimate farmers," he said. "If you give them a truck and a couple of ropes, they can get anything unstuck."

I studied the car for a while. Even with only a streetlight to see by, I saw the mud caked wheels and fender wells. There didn't seem to be any real damage.

"I promise I'll wash it tomorrow."

"And I'll help," Jim said.

George jumped up from his place under the table and stretched. He let out a small yip.

"Hush, George," Jim said. "You're pushing your luck."

"It's alright, Jimmy," Grandma said.

I caught a glimpse of Mr. Martin pushing his way toward the kitchen. He gave a quick wave to three men dressed in white coveralls, and they followed him out the back door.

Before I had a chance to ask what they were up to, Grandma turned toward the crowded room. She picked up her empty coffee cup and banged on the side of it with a teaspoon. The room got quiet immediately.

"It's been a rather long day," she said. "Shirley and I want to thank you for all your help."

"You don't have to thank us, Mrs. Ivey," someone in the back of the room said.

"Yeah, that's what neighbors are for," someone else said.

"Yip."

George's tongue hung from a corner of his mouth, and he looked as if he were smiling at me. I smiled back at him.

"Now, I would like all of you to join Shirley and me—and George," she said. "As you know, my birthday surprise for Shirley is waiting in the high school parking lot."

Forty-two

Grandma and I were so busy the last few weeks of my stay in Willowdale every workday went by in a blur. But on Sundays, Mr. Martin took us for picnics at Lake Sullivan or for drives in the countryside.

Pastor Lawrence was too busy practicing for the youth choir's fall schedule to take us back to the meadow with the fountain. Instead, he promised to take us next summer to see what he wanted to show us the day we got lost.

The potluck was such a success it was the main topic of conversation in Willowdale for the rest of the summer. The thunderstorm passed through the area so quickly the fireworks went off as scheduled, and they were enjoyed by everyone in the county.

"I can't believe it's my last night in Willowdale," I said to myself. "I just wish Jim would hurry up and get here."

I was at the bottom of Grandma's driveway in total darkness waiting for him, but I didn't have to wait very long. Within a few minutes, he drove up in his father's truck and pulled to a stop in front of me.

"Hey, Shirley."

"Hi, Jim."

I got into the truck and eased the door closed. I didn't want to make any loud noise and risk waking up Grandma.

"I just can't get over the people in Willowdale," I said. "I bet none of my friends ever had a town throw them a potluck dinner and shoot off fireworks."

"Probably not," he said. "Were any of them born on July fourth for crying out loud?"

It was late, and we were both tired from working all day. I understood why he was a little testy.

"No," I said.

"There you have it."

I looked back at the bed of the truck and counted the cans of paint. I hoped Jim brought enough, but we wouldn't know until we got up there.

"Explain to me again why we're doing this," he said.

"I want to do something special for Willowdale before I leave tomorrow."

"Why?"

I already explained my plan to him. I didn't understand why I needed to do it again.

"I want to do something special to thank everybody for being so nice to me this summer."

"Nobody expects any thanks, you know."

"I know," I said. "Let's get going."

He snapped on the truck's headlights and headed toward town. As we picked up speed, I looked back at Grandma's farmhouse. I was worried she heard me sneak out the back door, but there weren't any lights on anywhere.

"Thanks for helping me do this."

"Sure."

The cab was so stuffy I rolled down the side window, leaned back and let the warm air blow in on me. It was a hot August evening, and I was glad I wore shorts and a sleeveless blouse.

"Why are we doing this in the middle of the night?"

"Because I don't want anybody to know who did it."

Jim scratched his head, and for several seconds he drove without speaking. Finally, he looked over at me.

"Does that make any sense?"

"It makes perfect sense."

"It does?"

"If they knew it was us, it wouldn't be special anymore."

"Girls," he said. "I'll never figure you out."

"Anyway, I couldn't do it without your help."

When we got to town, Jim turned off the headlights and eased the truck down Main Street. There was only a sliver of the moon showing, but the streetlights and the light on top of the water tower were enough. We had no trouble finding our way.

"Did you remember the rope and the brushes?" I said.

"I brought everything you had on your list."

"Good."

We drove around the block and down the alley behind Grandma's café. A patch of grass within the round shadow of the water tower was out of sight of any businesses. Jim stopped there.

"This is the perfect place to hide the truck," I said.

He turned off the engine and watched the street for anyone who might be driving through town. I checked the immediate area for any movement, but I didn't see any.

Everything near us was hidden in the tower's shadow, and like a halo, the catwalk on the tower cast a circular shadow around it all. I hoped it was a good sign.

"How did you get out of the house without your grandmother seeing you?"

"I waited until she went to her bedroom for the night," I said. "George was already asleep, so it was easy to sneak out."

Jim sat quietly for a few seconds. It was too dark to see his face clearly, but I could sense he had something on his mind.

"It was really neat Aunt Maude asked me to keep George, don't you think?"

"I've been worried about that," I said. "You didn't know if you could afford to keep him."

He twisted in the seat and faced me. I still couldn't see his face clearly.

"Dad and I figured it out."

"You did?"

"Yep," he said. "Dad's going to trade milling time for dog food from the feed and grain store in Monticello."

"That's wonderful."

"And your grandmother said she'd save scraps for him."

I laughed. Grandma always had a soft spot in her heart for the little pug.

"But what if he gets sick or something?"

"Dr. Thompson."

"Dr. Thompson isn't a veterinarian."

"Doesn't matter," he said. "He wants to help out anyway."

I thought about our rivalry over George. As much as I wanted to take the little dog home with me, I finally realized how selfish that was. George was still the unofficial mascot of Willowdale. It would be wrong to take him away from the small town and all his human friends.

"I'm glad Aunt Maude picked you," I said.

"You really mean it?"

"I really do."

I looked out across the empty lot beside the café to deserted Main Street and all the darkened store fronts. My heart beat so fast, I was afraid it might burst.

Sneaking out of the house in the middle of the night and meeting Jim wasn't at all like me. Until that night, the most daring thing I ever did was wear a pink blouse with a red plaid skirt.

"And how did you get away from your house without your dad seeing you?"

"Basically, I snuck out."

"Your dad didn't see you load the truck?"

"Nope," he said. "He was on the phone, and I pretended I went to bed."

"But won't he miss all this paint?"

"He hasn't looked at any of this stuff for at least a couple of years."

"Good."

We both checked up and down Main Street and the alley one last time for any signs of life. I couldn't see lights in any of the buildings in our part of town, and there wasn't another car or truck in sight.

The way was clear, and the timing was right. I nodded at Jim.

"Are you ready?"

"I guess so."

"Then, let's go."

Forty-three

It was Sunday morning and my last day in Willowdale. It was too hot for a trip to the cemetery, but there were some things I needed to do before I left for home.

Mr. Martin pulled Grandpa's truck to the side of the road and parked next to Mr. Spencer's truck near the cemetery's entrance. The cab was empty.

It was too early for the main gate to be open, so the three of us searched for the place where Jim got inside. After a few minutes, Grandma found a missing upright in the wrought-iron fence. It was well hidden behind a row of juniper bushes.

One at a time, we squeezed through the opening, but it took me a little extra time to convince George to follow us. When he finally stepped through the fence, he looked up at me and wagged.

"That wasn't so bad, was it?" I said to him.

By that time, Grandma was well ahead of George and me. I tried pulling on the leash to hurry the little dog along, but he refused to speed up. He plodded along beside me at his usual snail's pace.

Grandma stopped in the shade of a weeping willow half-way up the gravel service road to look back at us. George and I lagged behind her by several yards, but Mr. Martin was even farther behind, clutching a bouquet of yellow roses from Grandma's flower garden.

"Don't dillydally, Shirley," she said. "Jimmy's waiting for us."

At the sound of Jim's name, George lunged forward against his leash. I struggled to hold onto the clothesline with my left hand and a paper shopping bag in my right hand.

"Okay, okay, big guy," I said. "I think that's fast enough this morning."

Jim and I didn't finish painting the water tower until two o'clock that morning. Fortunately, I was able to sneak back into the house without being seen, and I didn't have to explain what I was up to. But my shorts and blouse were too splotched with red paint to wear again. I tossed them into the kitchen garbage before going upstairs.

After only four hours of sleep, I was beyond exhausted. Who knew it would take Jim and me so long to finish the job? And who knew it would be such hard work?

"That's alright, George," I said. "Doing something nice for Willowdale was worth it."

I looked over my shoulder at the water tower poking its head above the trees in town. I couldn't help but smile. The bright red lettering practically glowed in the morning light.

"You don't look sad anymore."

George pulled harder on the leash, and I grimaced in pain. My hand wasn't the only thing that hurt. My back, my legs, my arms and my neck all screamed at me.

"You're so slow today, Shirley," Grandma said. "Is every-thing alright?"

"Everything's—fine."

She turned around and started up the road again. I stopped to check on Mr. Martin.

He wasn't behind us anymore. He was on a footpath lead-ing downhill toward the opposite side of the cemetery.

"Looks like it's just us, big guy," I said. "Let's take a short cut."

I stepped off the gravel road and pulled the little dog along with me. After only a few steps on the brown grass, George stopped short. His right front paw was suspended in midair above the parched grass, and he refused to move.

"What's the matter?" I said. "Does it hurt your feet?"

His wide eyes looked up at me. His tail hung straight down.

"I suppose I can carry you one last time."

As if I were a person four times my age, I bent down with a grunt and scooped him into my arms. With him tight against my chest and the shopping bag swinging from the crook of my elbow, I walked around one headstone after another.

When we finally reached the top of the hill, Jim and Grandma were waiting for us inside the gazebo. They sat on a wooden bench in the center of the structure where the shade was the deepest.

"I see you finally made it, my dear."

"Hey, Shirley."

Without a word, I knelt at the entrance and placed George on the ground. He thanked me for the ride by ignoring me and slogging over to Jim.

"You're welcome, big guy."

Jim slid off the bench, sat beside George and gave the little dog a long hug. Seeing them together made me want to cry, but I promised myself I wouldn't do that.

Grandma pulled a handkerchief from under the belt at her waist. She mopped at the perspiration on her forehead and upper lip.

"Ye gods, it's hot."

I grunted again when I stood up and took a place on the bench next to Grandma. The effort of carrying George up the hill was almost more than my aching body could bear.

I yawned and dropped the shopping bag. It landed with a thud at my feet.

"Tired, Shirley?" Jim said.

"Not at all," I said and yawned again.

"I'm going to take really good care of George," he said. "You can see for yourself when you come back next summer."

"I'll be checking, you know."

"I know."

"Don't you worry, dear," Grandma said. "We'll all look after him."

I tried to stop the tears, but I was powerless against them. They flooded my eyes and burst over my bottom lids. To keep Jim from seeing me cry, I slipped off the bench and sat on the other side of George. I cupped his face in my hands and kissed the top of his wrinkled head.

"Be a good boy for Jim," I said. "I'm really going to miss you."

When the little pug wagged his tail and stared at me, the tears came faster. I wiped at them with the back of my hand and sniffed.

"Thanks for coming with me, Grandma," I said. "I couldn't have brought George here by myself."

She handed me her handkerchief, and I dabbed at the tears. When the flow finally eased, I blew my nose.

"I understand how hard this is for you," she said. "But the train will arrive soon, and I think we should get started."

"Okay."

I struggled to stand up. Then, I picked up the shopping bag and left George with Jim. I reached out to Grandma, and she put her hand in mine.

"Thank you for letting me meet Jim here," I said. "I wanted to visit Dad before I left."

"Nonsense," she said. "I should have thought of it myself."

We walked, hand in hand, to two tall headstones not far from the gazebo. One was for Grandpa. The other was for my father. Grandpa's was still shiny, but Dad's was stained brown from sixteen years of weathering.

"Hi, Dad," I said. "Hi, Grandpa."

I let go of Grandma's hand and placed the shopping bag on the ground. I reached inside and pulled out two red roses I cut from her flower garden. One I laid on the base of Grandpa's stone. The other I laid on my father's.

"I wish Dad could hear me."

"I believe he does."

I looked over at her. Her eyes were full to the brim with tears, but her chin was jutted upward.

"You think so, Grandma?"

"I do, and I know he's very proud of you."

"Really?"

"Never doubt that for a moment."

It was overwhelming to think he could be proud of me even though he died in a car accident a few days after I was born. At the very thought, my tears flowed again, and I wiped at them with Grandma's hankie.

"Do you think I'll see him someday?"

For a moment, Grandma didn't say a word. Then, she turned toward me.

"What do you think?"

"I think I'll see him in Heaven."

"Then, you will," she said, "but not for many, many years."

I swallowed hard and reached into the bag once more. I used both hands to pick up the manila envelope. It was heavy with all the letters I wrote all summer.

"I wrote Dad nearly every day," I said. "It's kind of a journal so I won't forget anything about this summer."

"That was an excellent idea."

I put the envelope back inside the bag and pulled out my savings account book. The day was unbearably hot, but I needed to explain something to Grandma.

"Remember the day you made me open this account?"

"Of course."

"At first, I didn't understand about watching pennies," I said. "But I saw the balance grow bigger and bigger."

"It's an important lesson to learn."

"I was saving for the class sweater and ring."

"Yes, I remember."

"Then, I thought about something Jim said to me on our first picnic at Lake Sullivan."

"What in the world did he say?"

"He wanted to know what I was going to do with the money I earned this summer."

"What did you tell him?"

"I was impressed with how he plans to pay his own way through college, and I let him think I was working to pay for my college, too."

"Oh, I see."

"I didn't want him to think I was just some scatterbrained girl."

"No, you wouldn't want to do that," she said with a grin and a small chuckle.

"But it made me think."

"Think about what?"

"Priorities," I said. "I've decided not to get the ring and sweater after all."

"You have?"

"I've decided to save the money for college instead."

Grandma reached out and touched my arm. Her hand was trembling.

"That makes me very proud, indeed," she said.

I sniffed back more tears and dropped the bankbook inside the bag. I knew my friends wouldn't understand, but I didn't care. What my family thought of me was more important.

I stood up straight and scanned the cemetery. Jim was visiting his mother's grave only a few yards from us. George was in the shadow of her headstone, sleeping.

Mr. Martin was at the bottom of the hill, and the bouquet of yellow roses was on his wife's grave. Her headstone was flush against the ground and nearly the same color as the scorched lawn.

"I know I'll be driving for you next summer, Grandma, but what about this winter?"

"Jimmy has agreed to drive for me after school and on the weekends," she said. "In exchange, he will use the truck for delivering his papers."

"What about the rest of the time?"

"I see no reason why Mr. Martin can't drive in town during daylight hours."

I nodded my head in agreement. Mr. Martin didn't like me very much because I was a city girl, but he was Grandma's friend. I knew he would take good care of her and the truck while I was away.

In the distance, I heard the high-pitched whistle of the northbound train. The flag stop wasn't a very long drive from the cemetery, but I didn't want to be late.

"We'd better get going, Grandma."

I gave Dad's headstone and the rose one last look, grabbed the shopping bag off the ground and hooked my arm around Grandma's elbow. We slowly followed the long, winding service road down the hill to the entrance. By the time we got there, Jim and George and Mr. Martin were waiting outside the fence for us.

Grandma and I squeezed back through the opening, and Jim held the passenger door of Grandpa's truck open while Grandma climbed inside. Mr. Martin took his place on the driver's side.

While they settled in, I swung the shopping bag into the bed of the truck. I climbed in after it and sat down on the edge of my suitcase.

Jim waited until I was comfortable and lifted George up to me so I could say goodbye. I scratched the little dog behind his ears and gave him another kiss on the top of his head.

"See you next summer, George."

"We'll both see you next summer," Jim said and smiled at me.

With the little pug tucked under his arm like a football, Jim walked over to his father's truck and slid into the cab. As he drove away in the direction of the mill, he waved at me through the driver's window. George was on his lap, staring straight ahead.

When George didn't look back at me, I realized I was only a footnote in his life's story. I knew in my heart he belonged in Willowdale, but knowing that didn't make my feelings hurt any less. My eyes filled with tears again, and I blew my nose.

"Ya ready back there?" Mr. Martin said.

"I guess so."

What else could I say? My heart was breaking. I already missed Willowdale, and I wasn't even gone.

While he turned the truck around, I craned my neck to watch Jim and George make their way up Cemetery Road. In less than a minute, they rounded a curve and disappeared from sight.

There was nothing I could do but accept my fate and tidy up my appearance for my train ride home. I brushed at the wrinkles in the skirt of my cotton dress until my hand hit something sharp.

"What in the world is that?"

I lifted the hem of the skirt and found a small envelope pinned to the side of my canvas bag. It was addressed to me, so I unpinned it and ripped it open. Inside was a note in Grandma's handwriting.

"I am so proud of you and Jimmy," she wrote. "The water tower looks wonderful, and I rescued the clothes you threw in the garbage. If I am able to remove the red paint, they will be here for your visit next summer."

I smiled and shook my head. Carefully, I refolded the note and stuffed it back inside the envelope.

"Small towns and grandmas," I said to myself. "A person can't keep anything a secret."

About the Author

Carla J. Underwood was born in Indiana and grew up in a small town in the northwest corner of the state. She learned both the challenges and the rewards of living in a small community.

She embraced the small-town ideals and chose not to attend one of the large universities in Indiana after high school. Instead, she opted for a small university outside the state with a close-knit community of students. She earned her B.A. degree in Speech Pathology and Audiology there.

She and her husband are the parents of two children and the grandparents to six. They live in a small town in the desert Southwest and share their home with their nine-year-old pug.

www.ingramcontent.com/pod-product-compliance
Lightning Source LLC
Chambersburg PA
CBHW050718180626
46814CB00002B/490